UNSTOPPABLE

UNSTOPPABLE

TIM GREEN

HARPER
An Imprint of HarperCollins*Publishers*

Thirty percent of the royalties from the sale of this book will go to support the Center for Survivorship, a nonprofit organization founded by Jeffrey Keith and dedicated to empowering cancer survivors to live healthier, happier, and longer lives. You can visit them online at www.ctchallenge.org.

Unstoppable

 For information address HarperCollins Children's Books, a division of HarperCollins Publishers, 10 East 53rd Street, New York, NY 10022.
www.harpercollinschildrens.com

Library of Congress Cataloging-in-Publication Data is available.
ISBN 978-0-06-208956-4

Typography by Joel Tippie

12 13 14 15 16 LP/RRDH 10 9 8 7 6 5 4 3

First Edition

For my unstoppable wife, Illyssa

CHAPTER ONE

HARRISON ADMIRED THE NFL football player, battered and exhausted but unstoppable. Harrison knew about being battered and exhausted, not by the game, but by life. The player looked like a gladiator. Harrison looked like an overgrown farm kid. The player wore a green uniform with silver eagles' heads on the sleeves. Harrison looked down at his own stained and dirty coveralls and the worn-down boots poking from beneath tattered cuffs.

Sweat matted the player's long blond hair and beard. Blood ran down his face, but a light still shone in his eyes. Ghosts of steam curled up from his bare arms in the chilly night air. Skin slick with sweat stretched tight over bulging muscles. The crowd roared its cheers, urging the player and his teammates on to deeds of greatness. Harrison ached to be a football player and for people to cheer him on, but he never could, and they never would. Every day when the final school bell rang, instead of joining the other boys for football practice, Harrison hurried home for chores.

The player on the big-screen TV rammed a helmet down on his head, and the camera followed him out onto the field where he crouched, waiting. When the other team ran a sweep to the outside, the player swooped in like a real eagle, striking the runner, hitting him low and lifting him into the air so that he flipped and crashed to the turf. The player flexed his bare arms and stomped across the field in a parade of glory. The crowd went wild and Harrison couldn't keep still. A small, satisfied grunt escaped his lips.

Mr. Constable pounded his beer can onto the coffee table, spun around on the couch, and glared. "What are you doin' here, Mud?"

Harrison stepped back into the shadow of the doorway. Mr. Constable had called him "Mud" since the day he arrived. That didn't keep Harrison from continuing to think of himself as Harrison, and he threatened the two younger kids, Flossy and Crab, into calling him Harrison in private, even though Dora and Lump, the two older kids, called him Mud.

"I said 'what'?"

Harrison jumped and knew to answer. "Watching."

"You got chores. You don't watch." Mr. Constable raised a fist to prove it. The other hand crept toward his belt.

Harrison nodded, retreating toward the front door of the old farmhouse. Mrs. Constable appeared at the top of the stairs, her hair pulled so tight against her head that her forehead shined like a clean dinner plate. She puckered her lips and shook her head in disgust.

"Shoo!" she said, as if he were a big rodent.

Harrison returned to the barn and found his rusted shovel leaning in the doorway. A single bulb swung from the rafters, pushed by a small breeze. A cow shifted in one of the sick stalls. Her hooves scratched the dry hay. With the shovel in hand, Harrison dropped down into the milking parlor and the soup of manure. Green, brown, yellow—it depended on the feed the cows had taken. Harrison remembered the first time he'd smelled it, and the taste of vomit in the back of his throat.

Shadows flickered in the back corner of the parlor, and Harrison heard the hiss of hoses as Dora and Lump sprayed down the last of the milking machines. He began to shovel, slowly working the soup into the concrete channel and then down the channel until it disappeared into the night, plopping into the spreader below with a sloppy sound Harrison could sometimes hear in his sleep. The smell of cigarette smoke brought with it Cyrus Radford. The orange ember on the tip of the cigarette glowed in the doorway like the single eye of an angry little goblin before Cyrus stepped into the light.

"Where you been, Mud?" Cyrus wore coveralls like Harrison, also spattered with manure, but with no

T-shirt underneath to cover the leathery skin draped over his raggedy bones. He scratched the gray-and-black stubble on his chin and spit on the floor.

"Mr. Constable called me into the house." Harrison didn't like to lie, but it was better than a beating.

He knew Cyrus wouldn't question him being called into the house by Mr. Constable. Even though Harrison suspected that Cyrus hated Mr. Constable as much as any of the kids, Cyrus would never show it. Cyrus was afraid of Mr. Constable just like the rest of them. Who wouldn't be? Mr. Constable was a giant, thick and strong and rumbling with anger at everything life put down before him. His blond hair had begun to fade, but his face was as red as a baby's. His blue eyes were so pale, they sometimes seemed to glint back at Harrison like mirrors, making Mr. Constable seem something more, or less, than human.

"Well, finish up." Cyrus raised an arm to scratch at the hair in its naked pit. "It's late and I need a drink."

Cyrus Radford lived alone in a trailer resting on cinder blocks down by the main road. He supervised the milking at five in the morning, noon, and eight o'clock at night. Dora —who was sixteen—and Lump—fifteen—had the job of slipping the suction cups onto the cows' udders as they crowded into the milking parlor. Only Cyrus was allowed to remove the milking machines because Mr. Constable didn't trust any of his kids to know when the cow was completely empty. Harrison's job was to keep the barn clean, an unending and impossible task in a world of manure, dirt, and flies.

The younger kids helped Mrs. Constable around the house, and Harrison didn't envy them, because even though his job was dirtier and smellier, the younger kids were much closer to the tattered end of Mr. Constable's belt. Mr. Constable believed in his belt, just as he believed children needed hard work in order to improve. As the foster father of dozens of kids over the years, Mr. Constable said that was his mission in life, to improve wayward young people in order for the world to be a better place.

Harrison shoveled harder, trying to make up for the time he'd spent watching *Monday Night Football* from the doorway, scraping the concrete and spattering the manure so that tiny droplets speckled his face. Sweat dripped from his nose, and his older foster siblings had already disappeared when he heard Mr. Constable cough from the barn door. Harrison shoveled double-time, scraping and scratching and spattering, because he had a bad feeling about Mr. Constable's huge frame filling the doorway.

"Mud!"

Harrison looked up. Cyrus bobbed behind Mr. Constable—just beyond the lightbulb's reach.

"Yes, sir?"

"You been lyin', boy. You been lyin', again."

Mr. Constable removed the belt and flicked it against the concrete floor with a snap.

CHAPTER TWO

CYRUS DANCED A JIG behind Mr. Constable. Cyrus always liked to watch when Mr. Constable went to work. Cyrus did his share of beating the kids, but he didn't seem to delight in it the way he did when Mr. Constable used the belt. Maybe because Cyrus's switch didn't leave the deep, dark bruises that followed the lick of a belt.

"Ain't you?" Mr. Constable flicked the belt in the air with another expert snap.

Harrison nodded. Tears welled up in his eyes, but they weren't tears from fear; they were tears of rage. He didn't deserve the belt for sneaking a peek at the football game. He did his work, harder than the rest. He could lift two bales of hay at the same time and toss them up onto the back of a truck like they were sacks of groceries. So the fact that he would feel the sting of the belt made him want to explode. His fists clenched, and for the first time in the thirteen long years of his life, he thought about using them against an adult.

He had used his fists against other kids, plenty. That's what landed him at the Constables' home in the first place. It was the fourth foster home he'd been passed on to—passed on for fighting with other children. But it wasn't the kind of fighting people thought it was. Harrison fought for survival. Sometimes he even fought for others, kids weaker and more frightened than him of the older kids who seemed to haunt their lives.

At his last home Harrison had bloodied the noses and blackened the eyes of two boys three years older than him. No one seemed to care that those same two boys had forced a little kid named Wally to lie down in the grass so they could pee on him. No one seemed to listen, only talk in quiet, hard voices about Harrison, comparing him to a zoo animal, an untamed and untamable beast. That's why he had landed with the Constables. Mr. Constable was known throughout the county as a foster father who could cure even the hardest of bargains. Harrison now knew why.

CRACK!

Harrison turned and looked to the opening at the other end of the barn, but where would he run? He'd run before and knew that it only led to hunger, cold, and ultimately a ride home in the back of a police car before someone "whipped some sense into you."

"Don't you even look at me like that, boy. Mud boy. You came from mud and you'll return to mud. That's how I named you. Don't be flashin' those angry eyes at *me*. I'll put the lights right out of 'em."

Harrison let his shoulders sag.

"That's better. Say you're sorry to Mr. Radford here."

Cyrus held still and wore the blank look of disappointment. An apology had absolutely no entertainment value for Cyrus.

"I'm sorry, Cy—Mr. Radford."

"That's better." Mr. Constable threaded the belt back into his pants. "And you can thank your lucky stars we got to see the judge tomorrow; otherwise I'd be tanning your sorry hide. Don't you think I gone soft."

"The judge, sir?" Harrison tried to keep the hope from seeping into his voice. Mr. Constable didn't like the sound of hope.

"Just got a call from the lawyer. Seems your momma's got some funny notions again. Raised a ruckus at the county offices on Friday. Won't come to nothin'. Never do. Finish up. Take a bath so you don't smell for the judge. Then get to bed. I won't even ask you to stop lying. It's just in your nature." Mr. Constable turned and shuffled off into the darkness.

Cyrus checked over his shoulder before he stepped into the barn, picked his own willow switch from its place on the wall, and smacked it against Harrison's rump. Harrison spun with his fists clenched again. The grin on Cyrus's face went out.

"That's the last time." The words came out of Harrison's mouth without him even thinking. "You do that again and I'll be on you like stink on a cow patty."

Cyrus's mouth fell open and he pointed the switch at Harrison. "You get back to work before I tell Mr. Constable what you're up to. You think you're gettin' outta here from some judge? Your momma's a tramp and a druggie. She cast you off like garbage, and once a woman does that there ain't a judge in creation hands her back her kids, so don't you get so smart."

Harrison stared at Cyrus for a minute, until the older man blinked; then Harrison took up his shovel and got back to work. His hands shook as he shoveled and replayed the scene that had just occurred over in his mind. He looked at his own arms, the thick cords of muscles, hard from work. His feet bulged out the sides of boots made for a full-grown man, and he realized that something had tilted the balance. He had been ready to fight Cyrus, not because he thought he'd get free, but because he thought he could win. At thirteen, he was as big and fast and strong as a weak man. Stronger, in fact, than a man as weak and meanspirited as Cyrus, and he knew in his heart that one part of the nightmare was over. A grim smile twisted his lips.

Harrison finished his work and shut out the light. A cow brayed at him from the herd that shifted and stamped quietly in their pen as he crossed the yard.

"Shush," Harrison said, still trembling at the exciting realization about Cyrus.

In the bath, he took special care to scrub beneath his nails, behind his ears, and between his toes. He didn't want to look or smell like a farm boy tomorrow. He would see the judge. He might even see his own mother. Cyrus's cruel words about her came back to him and his ears burned with shame and hate. Maybe that was why he had been ready to fight.

He lay down on the bed between his brothers: Lump, a boy who'd once been known as Michael, and Crab, who called himself Luke, until the belt won out. Sleep came hard for Harrison. Tomorrow was apt to be like every other day in his life, disappointing and hopeless. Yet, something told him that it might not.

It just might not.

CHAPTER THREE

MRS. CONSTABLE BOUGHT CORNFLAKES in plastic bins the size of garbage cans. She had an old coffee cup on a string that she used to serve out a full scoop to each of the kids every morning for breakfast. And, despite the fact that the farm produced fresh milk every day, Mrs. Constable filled her kids with the powdered milk she got for free from the county. Harrison hated that soapy-tasting pale blue liquid, but he was hungry enough that he'd eat it on his cereal without a word of complaint, and he supposed that the words Mrs. Constable sometimes muttered to herself were true.

"Don't need to waste good milk on kids like these."

After breakfast, Mrs. Constable sent him back upstairs to wash behind his ears again. When he returned, she took her scissors out of the sewing drawer and told him to sit still on the kitchen stool so she could cut a straight line around his head just below the ears. Harrison did his best not to move, but still Mrs. Constable managed to nick an ear. She handed him a paper towel to stop the blood, and Harrison tried to whisk the tiny pieces of cut hair free from his neck, where they'd settled into the collar of his only white button-down dress shirt.

Mr. Constable appeared in his work clothes, ordered half a dozen fried eggs from his wife, and disappeared up the stairs to change into his brown suit. As Harrison cleaned up the mess from his haircut, he couldn't help sniffing the air as the eggs crackled in their puddles of butter. He knew if he was sly enough, he'd get to lick Mr. Constable's plate before it made its way into the sink for cleaning. Harrison laid his plans as he swept the kitchen floor. By working slow, he was able to delay long enough that he could fill Mr. Constable's coffee cup, then clean out the grinds from the pot, working slowly again, and offering to clean up the table.

"Don't you mess that shirt." Mrs. Constable glared over the tops of her glasses, and Harrison wondered how just the thought of a dirty shirt could make someone so angry.

"I won't. You want me to clean the dishes too, ma'am?"

"The boy doesn't run from work, I'll say that." Mrs. Constable sniffed with pleasure. Even though she had a dishwasher, Mrs. Constable complained about the electricity it used and preferred one of the kids do them by hand.

"If he weren't such a godforsaken liar, he'd almost be worth somethin'." Mr. Constable jammed a piece of buttered toast into his mouth and chewed from side to side like one of his own cows.

Harrison made his move on the plate, removing it from the checkered tablecloth and hurrying to the sink, where he got in two quick licks before slipping it into the soapy water.

"Did you lick that plate?" Mrs. Constable's voice cut his ears like a razor.

"No, ma'am," Harrison lied without pause.

"You better *not*." Mrs. Constable removed the plate from the soap and smudged at it with her fingertip.

Harrison didn't ask why she cared whether the soapy water got the dribs of yolk instead of him. "No, ma'am."

After the scrape of his chair, Mr. Constable stood and belched and pulled on his suit coat. "Time. I'll be back, Mrs."

"You call him 'Papa,' you hear?" Mrs. Constable dropped the plate into the water and scowled. "That's how you address Mr. Constable with the judge. You forget that and I'll have a bar of soap to feed you before afternoon chores."

Harrison knew well the taste of laundry soap, and he had to admit that it was a good reminder to call Mr.

Constable "Papa." Harrison climbed into the bed of the pickup truck with Zip, the jug-headed yellow Lab. The truck jounced down the driveway, jarring Harrison's bones until the tires hummed on the smooth blacktop. The wind whisked through his shortened hair and Harrison flicked at the tiny brown pieces still clinging to his neck. Town held the county courthouse and several brick government buildings as well as the crumbling storefronts of the past hundred and fifty years. Once busy with trade from the railroad, they now sold nothing much more than yarn and used furniture. There were also two bars, a diner, and a nail shop, while the rest of the windows held FOR SALE signs behind their dusty glass.

The courthouse was a busy place, though. Just outside town a large modern prison housed the state's less dangerous criminals and offered up most of the good jobs for fifty miles around. Half the people in the courthouse seemed to be prisoners, and none of them was ever as glum as Harrison would be if he had to wear handcuffs and an orange jumpsuit. Mr. Constable's shoes clapped against the wood floor after they passed through a metal detector, and Harrison followed him to the back part of the courthouse, the new part with low ceilings, fake blond wood, and fluorescent tubes of light.

In a courtroom that looked more like a classroom to Harrison, the judge sat on a low platform behind his bench. A state flag drooped alongside the American flag, and a brass clock hung on the wall. Mr. Constable waved to the lawyer, and they sat down. Harrison scanned the room for his mother, but she wasn't to be seen. The judge scolded two teenage boys in orange jumpsuits before banging his gavel on the desk and watching them be ushered out by an armed guard. The boys looked scared, and the judge seemed satisfied with that.

Harrison tugged at the collar of his shirt, replaying all the things he'd done recently that might put him in the company of the imprisoned boys.

"Harrison Johnson."

The bailiff looked out over the courtroom. Mr. Constable leaned close. "Don't forget—'Papa.'"

Mr. Constable stood. Harrison did too, and followed his foster father to the front along with the lawyer, a greasy-looking man in a green suit with food stains on its sleeves.

"Melinda Johnson?" The bailiff craned his neck and Harrison turned his head, also scanning the room. "Ms. Johnson? Melinda Johnson?"

Mr. Constable spoke to the lawyer under his breath. "All this fuss and she's too drunk to show up."

The lawyer nodded as if it was just another expected part of his job.

Harrison's heart sank.

"Is Melinda Johnson here, or counsel for Ms. Johnson?" The judge looked up over the top of his glasses and glared out across the room, clenching his teeth until the cords pulsed in his neck. "I see. Mr. Constable, will you approach the bench with your ward and counsel, please?"

The judge looked at Harrison with distaste before turning his attention to the lawyer. "Mr. Denny, do you have the paperwork for this boy's adoption?"

The lawyer fumbled with his briefcase, nodding and winking until he came up with a thick packet of papers. "Right here, your honor."

"Then," the judge said, examining the papers, "given the trouble Ms. Johnson has caused in all this and her apparent lack of responsibility—as well as respect for this court, I might add—all leads me to believe that the best course of action for this young . . . boy is to make him the legal and permanent son of Mr. and Mrs. Brad Constable."

A look passed between Mr. Constable and the lawyer that Harrison didn't like. It was the look of two bank robbers who'd been invited into the vault. Harrison scanned the courtroom behind him again, feeling desperate and sensing that something very big was about to happen, something that would change the course of his life.

Something that couldn't be put right again.

Something very bad.

CHAPTER FOUR

MR. CONSTABLE TOOK AN oath.

The teeth in his big head had too much room between them to form a complete smile, but it was the closest thing Harrison could remember to one. At the clerk's desk, the grown-ups signed papers while Harrison stood in his stiff white shirt, the hair itching him to no end. Panic choked him and he was unable to voice the protest he felt certain he should be making.

Mr. Constable nudged him before Harrison realized they were all staring at him and waiting for him to speak.

"Isn't that right, Son?" Mr. Constable asked.

"Yes, sir."

Mr. Constable's smile tightened and his eyes seemed to radiate heat. "You don't have to call me that, Son.

Call me what you always call me."

"Yes . . . Papa."

For some unknown reason, that made the adults chuckle. The judge took the papers the lawyer handed to him, added his own signature, pronounced Harrison Johnson officially and legally to be Harrison Constable, and struck the desk with his mallet.

There was a ruckus at the back of the courtroom as someone forced open the doors with a shriek.

CHAPTER FIVE

HARRISON FELT HIS INSIDES melt like butter in a hot pan.

His mother's dark frizzy hair shot out from her head in all directions. She wore a long raincoat and Harrison didn't know what else besides a dirty pair of fluffy pink slippers. He could see the red in her eyes from across the room and the heavy bags of exhaustion they carried beneath them.

Liquid pain pumped through his heart.

"That's my baby!" Harrison's mother screeched as the bailiff and a guard held her arms. "You can't do that to *my* baby!"

"Order in this court!" The judge pounded and glared, but it had no effect. "Order, I said, or you'll be in contempt!"

"Nooo!"

Tears welled up in Harrison's eyes. He felt like a split stick of firewood, half shamed, half aching to hold her. He started toward his mother, but Mr. Constable's big hand clamped down on the back of his neck so that the nerves tingled in his head.

"Bailiff, remove that woman and take her into custody for contempt. I'll not have it in my courtroom. I'll *not* have it." The judge pounded a final time as they dragged her out. Then he cleared his throat, gave an accusing look to Mr. Constable, and asked the clerk for the next case.

Mr. Constable steered Harrison from the courtroom and all the way outside into the sunshine. A light breezed whispered through the trees, making the whole thing seem like a dream.

"Where's my mother?" Harrison asked.

"It's all right, Mud. You got a new mother now, Mrs. Constable. She's your mother by law."

It was too much. Having a complete and legal family should provide comfort and nourishment for his soul, but it didn't. Harrison thought of a snake he'd discovered under some boards behind the barn, a small snake that had swallowed a whole rat. It sat like a lump, helpless and unable to move for weeks, until it could finally digest its prey. He was that snake.

Harrison's new status seemed to include sitting up front in the truck. He leaned his head against the glass without feeling the bumps and bangs, even as they climbed the hole-filled driveway to the farm.

Mr. Constable slowed down by the barn. "Chores."

"What about school?" Harrison asked.

"You're excused for court."

"But we're done."

Mr. Constable reached across the seat and grabbed a handful of Harrison's trimmed hair at the back of his head, twisting it until his head thumped sideways against the dashboard. Mr. Constable moved his face close, also tilting it so they both looked at the world in the same knocked-over way. "You're done givin' me lip, you understand?"

Harrison nodded his head.

"Say it."

"I understand."

"I understand, sir."

"I understand . . . sir."

Mr. Constable turned him free. Harrison spilled from the truck, tripped, and fell to the ground.

"Chores." Mr. Constable reached across the seat and yanked the door shut. Harrison sat dusting himself off as the truck pulled away toward the house.

He didn't know all the reasons why Mr. Constable wanted to adopt him, but he knew without a doubt that it would somehow end in the Constables getting more money from some charity or government program. He knew all the kids on the farm had started out as foster kids, only to be adopted by the Constables for some unspoken reason. While they didn't seem to mind, Harrison had never—and would never—stop thinking of Melinda Johnson as his one and only true mother. He would no more think of himself as Harrison Constable than he would as Mud Johnson, let alone Mud Constable.

Cyrus's switch whistled through the air and snapped against the barn door. "I heard 'chores' mentioned. I'm busy with the vet. I need hay for the calves and I need it now."

Without speaking, Harrison got to his feet and headed for the hay barn. He loaded several bales onto a wheelbarrow and bounced it across the barnyard to where the veal calves sat tied to the little plastic capsules that kept them out of the rain. With a pitchfork, he broke down the bales and scattered hay at the feet of each calf.

Finished, he put the pitchfork over his shoulder and headed for the noise in the milk barn. When he arrived, he saw Cyrus and the vet down in the parlor working on a cow whose head had been clamped down between some bars. The cow was having a calf, but something had gone wrong and the men shouted and hurried back and forth. Mr. Constable stood at the railing above, looking down with a stem of grass in his teeth. He turned and scowled at Harrison.

"I said 'chores.'"

"I finished feeding the calves." Harrison couldn't

help but notice the cow's violent kick and the vet's quick movement to dodge it.

"No, you're lying again."

Harrison's face felt hot. "I'm not lying. I finished."

Mr. Constable pointed behind Harrison at the box stalls where they kept sick animals. "Them two sick calves ain't fed yet. Lying again. I said I won't have it, and I won't."

Mr. Constable started to loosen his belt.

"No." Harrison shook his head.

"No? I'll show you, no."

"*You* lied!" Harrison surprised himself as the shout rose above the braying cow and the excited men, who both looked up from the parlor. "You said for me to call you 'Papa.' That's a *lie*!"

Mr. Constable's belt whipped out at him—not the leather part, but the buckle itself, a treat only for the most special occasions. When it licked Harrison's forehead, blood spurted from his skin and one eye went dark.

Harrison wasn't exactly sure what happened after that. He knew he used the pitchfork, and he heard Mr. Constable scream in pain as two of the tines buried themselves in his leg. Why he flipped backward over the railing Harrison couldn't imagine, but he did. Harrison didn't blame himself for the cow. It was a wild cow, mad with pain from a bad birth, and Mr. Constable fell into it and the cow kicked him with all its might.

The crack of Mr. Constable's skull was what Harrison remembered most, like a cobblestone split by a heavy sledgehammer.

And then the blood . . . and the screams . . . and the words. In the madness, at one point Mrs. Constable grabbed his ears and pulled his face close to hers so she could spit her hot words directly in his face.

"You *killed* him!"

CHAPTER SIX

IT WAS THREE DAYS before a woman from the county found him, locked inside the abandoned silo, hungry enough for his stomach to hurt bad and so thirsty he wished he hadn't wasted his own pee. Still, when he saw the woman's face and those kind, sad eyes, he had enough moisture in his body to cry, so he knew he must not have been too bad off. She put a blanket around him and tucked him into the backseat of her car, where he bounced comfortably down the drive, staring at Cyrus's tilted trailer for what he somehow knew was the last time.

"They said you ran away." The woman looked at him in the rearview mirror. "The police looked for you everywhere. It was your foster sister Dora who told a teacher at school. She'd be locked up herself if I had anything to do with it—not Dora, your foster mother."

The woman's eyes burned like little campfires. "Not that I have anything to do with it, though."

Harrison nodded.

She took him to a doctor who looked at his eye and gently cleaned the dried blood from the gash Mr. Constable's belt buckle had left him with.

"He'll live." The doctor held Harrison's head in his hands and looked down into his eyes, first one, then the other, with a penlight. "And I don't think we'll lose the eye. It should be fine when the swelling goes down."

Harrison never thought about losing an eye.

After two fish sandwiches and three bottles of Gatorade, he was taken to the police station, where he talked for a long time to an officer who was as nice as the woman. After that, she drove him to a place behind a high fence and metal gates. He took a shower and was shown to a small bedroom, where he expected to find an orange jumpsuit like the rest of the prisoners wore. The stiff, dark blue jeans and soft cotton shirt surprised him, and he looked at that same woman—she called herself Mrs. Godfrey—in confusion. There was even underwear and a pair of sneakers that looked big enough to fit him.

"I'll close the door so you can change," she said. "Then you can give me the towel."

Harrison looked down at the towel around his waist and by the time he looked up, she was gone. Dressed in his new clothes, he sat down to wait. After a soft knock, Mrs. Godfrey stuck her head inside the room.

"You all right, Harrison?"

He nodded.

She took the towel from him.

"Am I in jail for a long time?"

Mrs. Godfrey looked around at the room with no pictures or lamps or rugs. "No, Harrison. You're not in jail . . . well, you're not going to be here for long; it's just temporary, and it's not really a jail. It's a juvenile center."

Harrison tried to believe her.

It was hard, but after several weeks of walks and talking and good food and safe nights, he trusted Mrs. Godfrey. She believed him when he told her the stories of how he'd gotten to the point he was at, four different homes over the years, fighting, and the truth about how his eye had been broken open and Mr. Constable was kicked by the cow.

When she announced to him one day that the judge had undone his adoption to the Constables, he believed her, even though it was hard to understand the part about Cyrus being a hero of sorts by swearing on Harrison's behalf and saying he acted in self-defense against Mr. Constable.

"I guess he hated the Constables more than me," Harrison said, as much to himself as to Mrs. Godfrey.

* * *

Several more weeks went by before Mrs. Godfrey appeared one morning with a very serious and very different look on her face. The two of them sat at a picnic table outside the center in a shady spot on the grass.

"Harrison, I am very sad to tell you this, but I have to tell you because you need to know."

A spark flared in the back of Harrison's brain. "My mother."

"Yes." She covered his hand with hers. "She's gone, Harrison. I'm very sorry."

"She moved away?"

Tears glistened in Mrs. Godfrey's eyes. Slowly, she shook her head. "No, gone. She passed."

"My mother?"

"I'm very sorry."

Harrison didn't cry. He just blinked at her and watched a tear roll down her nose and drop off the end of it, spattering onto the table where they sat.

"Was she sick?" he whispered, his eyes on the spattered drop.

"I think she was very sick, and very tired, and I think she's in a place now where she's at peace and watching you and loving you just like she always did."

Harrison stared at the broken tear for a long time before he spoke. "Mr. Constable said she didn't."

"Harrison, most people in this world are good, but some are bad. Mr. Constable was a very bad man, and he was a liar. That's all I can say about it."

They sat for a while before Mrs. Godfrey brought a hand to her mouth and cleared her throat. "Now I have some more news for you."

Harrison studied her eyes, afraid.

She patted his hand. "Good news, this time."

CHAPTER SEVEN

"TOMORROW YOU'LL BE GOING with a new family."

Harrison looked at his hands and sighed.

"I think you'll like them."

He looked up at her, unable to stop the anger from burning in his eyes. "That's what they always say."

She reached out and put a hand on his shoulder. "This will be different, Harrison. I promise. Did anyone ever promise you before?"

He scowled down into his lap. "Only my mother."

Mrs. Godfrey stayed quiet for a minute, and he thought she might be about to leave until she cleared her throat again. "Well, I'm different from your mother. I've been a lot luckier than she has, and because I've been so lucky, I've been able to keep my promises."

Harrison looked up into her eyes and saw they were

glassy, and her fuzzy top lip trembled ever so slightly. "*Every* time?"

"Yes, and even though you've been very unlucky, you have to believe me that there are many foster parents out there who are wonderful people who care very deeply for their children. This time, I promise that you're going to be with two *very* special people."

"How do you know?"

"She's my daughter."

"Who?"

"The place you're going. My daughter's. She's very nice."

"Like you?"

"Yes." She sniffed and let out a breath, then smiled and nodded. "And her husband is a very good man. They don't have any children of their own. I told them all about you, Harrison, and they'd like to help."

"Is it a farm?"

Mrs. Godfrey kept smiling. She sniffed again and looked off into the sky. "No, it's not a farm. He's a teacher and she's a lawyer."

"What does he teach?"

"English, and he's a football coach."

"Football?" Harrison felt a flame of excitement burst to life in his chest. "Do you think they'd let me play?"

"Well, Harrison, I know for a fact that he'd love it if you did."

CHAPTER EIGHT

RON KELLY PICKED HARRISON up at the bus station. He had a farmer's hands, rough and strong, but from working with weights and wood, not cows and tractors. His grip could crush stones, but his smile warmed Harrison's heart because it had just as much warmth as the smile he'd grown used to seeing on Mrs. Godfrey's face. He also didn't mind when Mr. Kelly asked Harrison to call him "Coach" because that's what he said all the students called him, whether they played football or not.

Mrs. Godfrey's daughter was waiting for them at home, a big gray house with white shutters and a bright-red front door. Coach's wife had long red hair. She wore thin glasses, but they couldn't hide her pretty green eyes, and her resemblance to Mrs. Godfrey was obvious when she smiled. Mrs. Kelly was a lawyer and Harrison could see why. Words flowed from her mouth like a song. Coach spoke more like a barking dog, and Harrison wondered how it was the two of them could get along so well, but they seemed to.

They showed Harrison his room and it was nice. While he studied it, Harrison caught Mrs. Kelly looking at his eye. He wanted to cover it because a thing so ugly didn't seem to fit in such a room. There were curtains on the windows. The bed sheets were crisp and white and the clothes in the closet were clean and ironed, without tears or stains. Beside the dresser stood a case of shelves bursting with books.

Harrison forgot about his eye at the sight of the books. Mrs. Kelly used a long finger to break one loose and she held it up for him so that he could see a serious young man's face on the cover, a sword in his belt, and his hand gripping a ship's rope as he looked out over the waves. On the distant shore, a rainbow rose from the land, arcing across the sky and promising good things to come.

"Have you ever read Louis L'Amour?" Mrs. Kelly asked.

Harrison shook his head, not wanting to tell her he'd never read a book, period.

"I think you'll like this." She handed him the book. "My brothers loved *The Sacketts.* It's a family that comes to America when it was a new land."

"I was a Hardy Boys guy," said Coach with a grunt from the doorway.

Harrison shifted his feet. He hadn't heard of them, either.

"Are you hungry?" Mrs. Kelly asked.

Harrison nodded.

He followed them downstairs. They all sat at the table, where Mrs. Kelly had lunch already laid out—sandwich meat, cheese, bread, and salad. Harrison watched, mystified as they bowed their heads and Coach uttered a prayer. Harrison's first two families said lots of prayers, but it had been many years since he'd heard them and the prayers hadn't done anything to make them nicer people. His face felt hot when Coach looked up and saw him gawking. Coach just smiled and passed the bread.

Harrison put together a turkey sandwich and doused it with ketchup.

"We hope you'll feel welcome, Harrison," Mrs. Kelly said, "and that you like your room."

"I do."

"You're a big kid," Coach said. "My mother-in-law said you might want to play some football?"

Mrs. Kelly rattled her butter knife against the plate. "Really, Ron? Football? Harrison hasn't been sitting for more than five minutes and you're already going there?"

Coach shrugged and scowled at his wife, but not in a

mean way. "He's a big boy and you know I need all the help I can get. Have you ever played before, Harrison?"

"No, but I like to watch it, and I think I could."

Jennifer flashed Coach a look, sharp as a knife. "Would you like some salad, Harrison?"

"Is it okay if I don't?" he asked, the green food looking like something he'd give to the cows.

"Of course."

"And I would like to play football, Mr.—I mean, Coach."

Coach grinned and slapped a hand on the table, jarring the silverware. "Then it's settled. Tomorrow after school I'll get you geared up and you can get started. No sense wasting time. You'll need ten practices before you can play in a game, but that means you can play in next week's game. This is great. You'll like the team."

Mrs. Kelly gave her husband an impatient look. "Coach has a lot riding on this season, Harrison, so you'll have to forgive his overexcitement."

"There's no such thing as overexcitement when you're talking about football," said Coach.

Mrs. Kelly continued as if her husband wasn't there. "The varsity coach is retiring after this season, and there are some people who'd like Coach to take over."

"But not everyone." Coach clenched and unclenched his jaw so that the muscles in his face did a dance.

"Not the head of the booster club," Mrs. Kelly said in a voice as light as the butter she spread across her bread. "He thinks we should find someone outside the program."

"I need to win the league," Coach said. "Then he can't say no."

"But we lost the first two games," Mrs. Kelly said.

"We should win this week," Coach said. "I haven't lost to East Manfield in ten years."

"You've never started out oh-and-two and made the playoffs." Mrs. Kelly bit into her slice of bread and sipped at a cup of tea. A dab of butter clung to her upper lip until she wiped it away with a napkin. "But winners never quit, and quitters never win."

"How fast are you?" Coach asked.

Harrison blushed and shrugged. He didn't know how to answer. As a little kid, he won all the races on the playground, and he was always good in gym class, but he'd never been allowed to play any sports. "Pretty fast, I think."

"Pretty fast, and big for sure." Coach seemed to speak to himself.

"He'll need a physical," Mrs. Kelly said.

Coach scratched the stubble on his head. "Maybe I could get Doc Smart to see him and give us a clean bill of health."

Mrs. Kelly pointed quickly to her own eye and said, "What about . . ."

"Your mom said his eye is fine. It just looks bad," Coach said.

Harrison knew from the mirror that what should be white in his eye was still bloodred, and that even though the swelling had been gone for several weeks now, the skin around his eyes was still marbled with purple and a sickly yellow.

"It's Sunday, Ron."

Coach waved a hand. "Doc won't mind. He's a friend. If Harrison wants to play, there's no sense in making him wait."

Mrs. Kelly sighed. "I guess you can ask."

CHAPTER NINE

COACH DROVE AN OLD white pickup truck. Rust crept along the underside of the doors, and the tires looked dusty and smooth. Riding through town, Harrison couldn't help admiring the neatly trimmed lawns and the old houses wearing coats of fresh paint. Doc Smart lived in a big house up a long driveway. A handful of kids played Frisbee on the lawn. They wore fancy clothes—shirts with collars, dresses, and shoes that reflected the sunlight. A pretty girl with a blond ponytail caught the Frisbee and stopped the game to watch Harrison follow Coach up the front steps and into the house. Harrison put a hand up to cover his discolored eye.

Doc Smart showed them into an office, where he poked and prodded Harrison.

"Let me take a look at that eye." The doctor shone a penlight at it. "Can I ask what happened?"

"Hit by a belt buckle," Harrison said.

Coach cleared his throat.

"It feels fine, though," Harrison said. He didn't want to wreck the whole deal before he even got started.

Doc Smart glanced at Coach and snapped off his light. "Well, it's healed up nicely. Shouldn't keep you from playing football."

Doc took Harrison's blood pressure and banged his knee with a rubber hammer, then signed some papers and told Coach that Harrison was ready for action. Doc followed them out onto the front porch and called to the ponytail girl. "Becky, I want you to meet Harrison. Harrison, this is my daughter, Becky. She's in your grade."

Becky held out her hand and Harrison shook it, surprised by her solid grip, even though his hand swallowed hers whole. He also liked the way she didn't stare at his red eye. It was as if she didn't notice, even though he knew she must have.

"Harrison is Coach Kelly's . . ."

"Harrison is joining our family." Coach put a hand on Harrison's shoulder and gave it a squeeze.

Harrison felt his face burn. Becky looked at him in confusion. Coach steered Harrison down the steps toward the truck. Harrison saw the other kids on the lawn watching him like a zoo animal. He climbed into the truck beside Coach. As they backed down the driveway, Becky stepped down off the porch. She caught Harrison's eye and then did something that he'd never forget.

CHAPTER TEN

WITH ALL THE OTHER kids watching, Becky waved to Harrison and spoke in a voice that all the kids could hear. "I'll see you in school, Harrison."

Her smile filled Harrison's heart with sunshine and honey, and his own hand popped up on its own to wave back at her.

"That's a pretty little girl." Coach nodded his head toward the doctor's daughter.

Harrison looked down at his feet and scuffed a gum wrapper across the floor mat.

"Don't you think?" Coach backed the truck out into the street.

"I don't know." Harrison studied the wrapper. His ears burned at the sound of Coach's soft laughter.

Coach settled down and asked Harrison if he wanted

to go fishing. Harrison said that he had never been but that he'd be happy to try. They returned home to get their gear, and while Mrs. Kelly packed a basket with sandwiches and lemonade, Harrison studied some framed photographs on a table in the living room. In one, Mrs. Kelly wore a wedding dress and Coach had on a tuxedo. In another, Mrs. Kelly hugged Coach on the sideline of a football field and Coach held up a trophy. Another caught Harrison's eye and he picked it up.

It was Coach, but he wore an Army uniform. In one hand he held a gun, but his other arm he'd slung around a second soldier. They smiled like brothers at a reunion. The other soldier had a small beard that was as black as his eyes, reminding Harrison of a movie poster he'd once seen for a story about the devil.

When Mrs. Kelly appeared behind him, Harrison returned the picture to its place.

"Coach was in the war?" he asked.

Mrs. Kelly handed Harrison the picnic basket. "The Gulf War. It was the first war in Iraq, a lot of years ago."

"That's his friend?"

"A very good friend," she said, looking sadly at the picture. "Major Bauer."

"Did he die?" Harrison kept his voice low.

Mrs. Kelly seemed to think about it. "No, he was hurt very badly, but he's far from dead. You'll meet him sometime."

Harrison could tell there was something special about the major that Mrs. Kelly wasn't telling him, but they both heard Coach call him from the garage, and she put a hand on Harrison's back and steered him toward the door. Coach laid two poles in the back of the truck, dusted his hands, and they set out for the lake. Coach had a boat with an outboard motor pulled up among some grass and trees on a rocky shore. When Coach asked Harrison to help him drag the boat into the water, Harrison grabbed hold of the handle in front and hauled it across the rocky beach and into the water before Coach could put down his basket and fishing gear.

Coach stared at him, and Harrison wondered if he'd done something wrong.

"With the motor, that boat weighs about four hundred pounds," Coach said.

Harrison looked at the boat and shrugged.

"Okay, great. Let's load it up." Coach set the gear and basket into the bottom of the boat. Harrison got in and Coach launched them into the deeper water and hopped aboard. The engine sputtered, then hummed. Coach steered for a point of rocks a ways away and dropped anchor at a spot where Harrison could see the stony bottom.

Coach handed Harrison a fishing rod before focusing on his own rig, fussing with the reel, breaking open a big plastic box, and tying a small metal fish lure dangling hooks onto the end of the line. Coach looked up and blinked at Harrison, nudging the box his way before he looked back down.

Coach looked up again. "I'm sorry. You said you never went fishing, and here I am giving you the tackle box. It's just second nature for me, that's all. You never even saw anyone fishing?"

"Just along the bridge on the Sawmill River, or on TV, I guess."

"Okay, sure. Here, let me tie one of these babies off for you." Coach took the pole Harrison held and expertly tied a curved golden fish onto the end of the line. The lure sparkled in the sunlight. "You just cast it toward those rocks and reel it in, like this."

Coach flicked his wrist and the lure on the end of his pole sailed through the air, plunking down not far from the rocks jutting out of the water. Immediately he began winding the handle, reeling in the line as fast as he could. Coach wore sunglasses beneath the brim of his "Bulldogs Football" cap, but Harrison could tell his eyes were locked on the spot where the lure had gone in. Magically, the end of the long pole bent once, then three more times, as if someone were tugging on it. Coach yanked the pole, quickly and viciously.

"Got 'em." A smile broke out on Coach's face, and now he reeled steadily against the flailing pole.

Harrison saw a flash in the water, then the fish broke the surface, twisting violently in the air before it dove back down, bending the pole even more.

"A beauty," Coach said. "How about that? First cast. Hand me that net, will you?"

Harrison held out the net. Several minutes later, when Coach had reeled the fish in and alongside the boat, he grabbed the net from Harrison without looking and expertly scooped the fish out of the water. "Supper."

Coach unhooked his catch and held it up by pinching its lower lip between thumb and forefinger. As he raised it up for Harrison to see, Coach sucked air in through his teeth. "Look at that. Wow."

Coach turned the fish so Harrison could see a set of diagonal gashes that ran up one side of the fish, ending at its tail. Its eye, like Harrison's, was bloodred. Part of the back fin was also missing. "Propeller got him."

Harrison wrinkled his forehead. "Are you gonna let him go?"

"Go?" Coach raised his eyebrows. "No, he can't last long like this, but he'll still eat good."

Coach reached into his tackle box and looped a bigger metal hook up through where the fish's bright-red gills strained for water to breathe and out its mouth. A dozen other big hooks dangled from the same chain. Coach called it a "stringer" and he attached it to a metal ring beside his seat before sliding the fish back into the water on its metal leash. Harrison peered over the side of the boat and watched the fish thrashing for a few moments before it settled into a lazy waving motion with its shattered tail.

"You want to try?" Coach asked. "I can't promise you'll catch one that fast. Lucky cast."

Harrison continued to stare at the fish. "I thought you let them go. That's what they do on TV."

"That's a bass tournament, sure, but I like to eat what I catch. Trust me, this one's better off on a plate. Didn't you ever see *The Lion King* and that whole 'circle of life' thing?"

Harrison shook his head and refused the pole Coach held out to him. "I can't."

"Harrison, things die. You eat hamburgers, right?"

He nodded.

"Yeah, well, someone had to kill a cow for you to eat that burger. That's how it goes, right?"

"But this one's hurt."

"Right, and hurt things don't survive. That's nature."

Harrison shook his head again. "When something's hurt, you're supposed to help it."

Coach looked around, but there was no one there to help him. "So we can catch healthy ones and keep them to eat? Is that okay?"

"Sure."

"You got a lot going on in there, you know that?"

Harrison shrugged.

Coach huffed and pulled the stringer up out of the water. "You want to let this fish go?"

"I don't want you to be mad," Harrison said.

Coach's face softened. "I'm not mad. I think I get it. You're a good kid, Harrison, you know that?"

Harrison eyed Coach with suspicion. Then his throat tightened and his eyes got moist.

No one had ever called him that before.

CHAPTER ELEVEN

THE INJURED FISH WAGGED its tail and disappeared with a flash among the sunbeams reaching deep into the water. Harrison felt a smile creep onto his face.

They kept fishing. Harrison tangled the line a couple times and botched most of his casts, but Coach didn't seem to mind. He was patient with Harrison, and after some time Harrison was able to cast pretty well. He never caught a fish, but Coach got three and laughed when Harrison nodded his approval to set them aside for dinner. None were as big as the injured one, but Coach said his wife would be happy.

Harrison didn't mind helping Coach clean the fish and he couldn't explain what bothered him so much about the hurt fish, but Coach didn't bring it up. Mrs. Kelly was happy, and she laid the long slabs Coach cut from the sides of the fish into flour before settling them into a pan that snapped with bacon grease and onions. Harrison's mouth watered; the fish was delicious.

After dinner, Harrison and Coach cleaned up while Mrs. Kelly sipped tea and worked on a puzzle set out in what looked like a million pieces across the dining room table in the next room. When they finished, Coach and Harrison helped with the puzzle until Mrs. Kelly yawned and looked at the clock. Darkness had enveloped the house not long after dinner, but Harrison was still surprised to see that it was already nine o'clock.

"We like to read before bed, Harrison. I know you might like to watch TV, but it's something we try to do only a couple times a week. Coach has his *Monday Night Football* and I like *Dancing with the Stars.* Is there a show you watch?"

Harrison shrugged. The Constables liked to watch TV, but he never got to choose the channel, and what they watched, besides football, never interested him. Lump, his older foster brother, had an old Game Boy, and Harrison used to watch him play it and was rewarded every so often when Lump let him have a turn. So, when Mrs. Kelly suggested that Harrison might like to read—as she said she and Coach would do—before bed, he figured it was worth a try.

Coach shook his hand and Mrs. Kelly kissed the top of his head at the landing on the second floor before turning down the long hall toward their own room.

Harrison used the bathroom—his own bathroom—that opened directly into his room. He marveled at the soap, smooth and pink and clean, nothing like the cracked and grimy cakes he was used to at the Constables' farm. The corners of the tub were white and clean too. There was no grease or grime or old, oily body hair.

He shuddered and stripped down to his boxers and looked at the fresh white sheets. Mrs. Kelly had turned the covers down so that a crisp white triangle welcomed him to the bed. *Sackett's Land* was the name of the book on the night table beneath a small lamp. Harrison climbed into the bed, propping himself up on two pillows, and opened the book.

The first words made him go cold.

CHAPTER TWELVE

"It was my devil's own temper that brought me to grief . . ."

Harrison looked around the room. A car drove by down on the street. He listened to it disappear and then to the quiet ticking sounds of the house. He thought he could just make out the murmur of Coach and his wife talking in their bed. Were they talking about him?

He had no doubt the first words of this book were meant to scold him for his past deeds and his own devil's temper that led to the death of Mr. Constable. Curious, he read some more.

". . . my temper and a skill with weapons born of my father's teaching."

He stopped again. That didn't fit him. No one had ever taught him anything about weapons, and certainly not his father. Harrison had no idea who his father was.

While the second part of the first sentence made him less certain the book was meant as a message to him, it made him even more interested to go on.

Harrison read, and read, and read.

He only stopped to look up at the sound of a soft knock on his bedroom door.

He laid the book on his chest.

The knock came again.

"Yes?" he asked.

The door opened a crack. Mrs. Kelly peeked in. "You like it?"

Harrison nodded. "There's a lot of fighting. With swords."

"Good. I'm so glad you like it, Harrison, and I hate to even say this, but it's getting very late and I just don't want you to be tired on your first day. Okay?"

"What time is it?"

"Just after midnight."

Harrison looked at the night outside his window. "Okay."

"Good night, Harrison."

"Good night, Mrs. Kelly."

Mrs. Kelly's head disappeared, only to reappear a moment later. "You don't have to call me Mrs. Kelly. It makes me think of Coach's mother. I know you might not want to call me Mom, although you're welcome to, but I'm guessing that may take some time."

"Mrs. Coach?"

That made her laugh. "Oh, no. Please, not that. How about Jennifer? That's my name."

"Would Coach be okay with that? I mean, you're a grown-up."

"I think Coach will love it. Good night, Harrison."

"Good night, Mrs.—" Harrison swallowed. "Good night . . . Jennifer."

"Very nice."

Harrison turned out the light and whispered her name twice to himself. As he lay alone in the dark, he thought about the story he had begun and about the main character, Barnabas Sackett. Then he thought about himself. Barnabas had found an old purse with gold coins that was the beginning of his fortune. Maybe tomorrow he'd find his own bag of gold coins. Maybe it would be the game of football, a thing he'd dreamed of for so long.

He imagined himself the star of the team, the boy everyone wanted to be, and he couldn't see that picture in his mind without the girl, Becky, standing beside him.

With that thought, and a smile on his face, Harrison slept.

CHAPTER THIRTEEN

THE NEW JEANS JENNIFER had put out for him were a little stiff, but the blue cotton shirt with its polo collar felt almost as soft as his bed sheets. Jennifer made eggs over easy with whole wheat toast. Before he ate, though, she boiled a clear plastic football mouthpiece, dipped it into cold water, and helped Harrison mold it to his teeth. He then tucked it into his pants pocket so that he wouldn't misplace it. Coach was all business, reading the paper and drinking two cups of coffee, before he stood with a clap of his hands. "Let's go, Harrison. School."

Harrison followed, accepting the brown bag lunch from Jennifer. He stuffed the lunch into a backpack she gave him that was already filled with notebooks, pencils, pens, and some empty folders. From the front seat of Coach's truck, Harrison stared at the kids walking to school, some in little clusters, others by themselves. Harrison studied their faces as best he could, looking for something they'd have in common and seeing nothing that would help him to fit in. His mouth dried out and his palms grew damp.

Coach turned off the truck in the parking lot beside the school. He reached into his briefcase and handed Harrison a packet of papers stapled together.

"It's our playbook. I don't want you looking at it during classes, but if you have time at lunch or study hall, you might want to take a look."

Coach flipped open the packet and pointed at a series of circles and Xs. "You see? This page shows you the number for each hole. Next are the formations, then after that the plays. The circle that's filled in is the guy who gets the ball. Then, these are our basic defenses, just where to line up. It's pretty simple, really, and if you have the chance to look it over, things will make sense out there."

Harrison held the packet like it was gold and tucked it into his backpack.

Coach walked him into the Brookton Junior High School office, introduced him to the principal, Mr. Fisk, and then sat him down in the office of Mr. Sofia, the guidance counselor. Mr. Sofia had a kind but worried face, and his dark hair had thinned enough that his tan scalp shone through. Mr. Sofia finally stopped staring at Harrison's discolored eye and went over his school schedule. Coach signed some papers. The bell rang as the three of them entered the hallway. Kids scrambled for their classrooms and no one paid Harrison any attention.

Coach stopped and turned to Mr. Sofia. "Frank, can I have a second with Harrison?"

Mr. Sofia nodded and disappeared around the corner.

Coach cleared his throat and looked around before he spoke in a low voice to Harrison. "I have to tell you something that's very important."

CHAPTER FOURTEEN

COACH LOOKED HARD AT Harrison, and Harrison dipped his head.

"I know about everything that happened in your old life, Harrison," Coach said, "and I believe my mother-in-law when she says you've just caught a bunch of bad breaks."

Harrison glanced up and saw that Coach meant what he said.

"Okay," Coach said, "fine. You'll get a fresh start here. But I also know kids, and I know what happens when a new kid shows up. You'll be the biggest kid in the grade, so you'll stick out, and your eye is still kind of noticeable, and I'll bet dollars to donuts that before the day is out someone's going to give you some grief. That's life.

"Well, I need you to rise above it. I can't have you exploding on me and knocking someone's block off. Do you get what I'm saying? You might get angry. I know it. But you've got to contain it. Save it up for football practice today. I promise, you'll get to let it all out then, but you've got to wait. You can't fight anyone, no matter what. You understand? If you have problems, you tell me and we'll work it out."

Harrison realized that Coach was staring at him, hard.

"Okay?" Coach asked.

"Okay."

Coach mussed his hair. "Good. I'll see you third period."

Harrison watched him go, then he went in the direction of the guidance counselor. When Mr. Sofia showed Harrison his locker and handed him the combination, they were the only people in the hallway. "Your . . . father . . . your foster father is a good man."

Harrison looked around and realized Mr. Sofia was talking to him. He didn't know what to say about that. It was hard to think of Coach as his father because the word had come to mean something Harrison didn't necessarily appreciate, and he already really liked Coach.

After Mr. Sofia realized Harrison had no reply, he pointed to a door down the hall. "There's your math class, Mrs. Zebolt, 209. If you have any problems or questions, you can stop by anytime."

"Thank you, Mr. Sofia."

The guidance counselor smiled a big, bright smile and said, "Kids call me 'S.' Just 'S.'"

Harrison nodded and crossed the hall to 209. He opened the door and stepped inside. All eyes were on him.

"You're late, young man." The teacher had little round glasses and the curly brown hair of a poodle. "That's no way to start your career with *me*."

Harrison said nothing. One empty desk remained in the front row. He sat down at it, but not before he saw Becky Smart sitting in the back. That only made Harrison's face glow, and he hunched over in the front seat, aware that he blocked the view of the person behind him.

"Your name?"

It took Harrison a moment before he realized the teacher was talking to him.

"Harrison."

"Harrison what?" she asked.

"Harrison Johnson, ma'am."

"Manners?" Mrs. Zebolt sniffed. "I know all about your past, Harrison."

Harrison nodded and felt his cheeks warm.

Mrs. Zebolt turned back to the whiteboard, attacking it with her marker in little squeaky bursts.

Harrison felt a pencil eraser poke him in the back. The boy behind him whispered, "Hey, you big, dumb retard. How many grades did you fail?"

Harrison shifted in his seat, ignoring the kid. He felt the anger building up inside him, but he remembered Coach's words only a few minutes ago. It almost seemed like Coach had set him up, to test him. That's what Harrison thought, and he was determined to pass the test.

After a few minutes, he felt another poke. "What are you, a retarded zombie? What's with that bloody eye, you retard?"

Harrison heard the boy next to him and the girl behind him snicker together under their breath and glance his way.

Harrison saw red. He had a vision of himself turning around and punching the boy directly in the mouth, breaking his teeth, and then throwing him to the ground for a good stomping. He actually could see it happening in his mind, but he brought Coach's words back to life in his head. He had to hold back.

But when the next poke came, Harrison couldn't help himself.

He had to do something, and he spun around.

CHAPTER FIFTEEN

INSTEAD OF FREEING THE punch that had coiled itself up inside his arm like a rattlesnake, Harrison snatched the boy's pencil and snapped it like a matchstick in one hand. He laid the broken pieces on the desk, ignoring the look of shock on the boy's face, and turned back toward the front.

Mrs. Zebolt's marker squeaked out the final line to her problem and only then did she turn to face the class. "Who can tell me how to solve this?"

Silence greeted her. She scowled and headed for Harrison, holding out the marker. "Well, Mr. *Johnson*, in case you're not the type to do your homework, it'll be good for you to know that if no one volunteers, I *choose* a person to do the problem. And, if they *can't*, it's an F that gets added into their test scores for the marking period."

Mrs. Zebolt was two steps from Harrison. The anger burning in him from being poked and teased was already simmering beneath his skin, and now this mean teacher was going to give him an F when he'd done nothing wrong?

The teacher took another step, then someone said, "I know the answer, Mrs. Zebolt."

All eyes turned toward Becky Smart. She was already up and out of her seat. She whisked past Mrs. Zebolt and stood facing the board. She stared for a moment, then began to jot down a series of numbers until she wrote "$x = 7/8$," circled it, and spun around.

Mrs. Zebolt stared and her lips worked through the series of calculations as if someone had hit her mute button. Then she squeezed her lips together before saying, "Correct."

Becky returned to her seat, offering Harrison a quick wink as she passed.

The boy behind Harrison muttered, "Beauty and the beast."

The pair next to Harrison giggled again.

"Do you have something to share with the class, Mr. Johnson?" The teacher glared.

Harrison shook his head.

"Then I suggest you take that angry look off your face," the teacher said. "It neither frightens nor intimidates me, despite the stories I've heard."

Harrison unclenched his teeth.

"And you, Mr. Howard?" The teacher looked past Harrison at the boy sitting behind him, allowing Harrison to turn and get a better look at his enemy. Howard was tall and thick-shouldered with short red hair, freckles, and a mean, pinched-up face.

"Me, what?" He scowled right back at the teacher.

"Do you have anything to share, Leonard Howard?" Mrs. Zebolt seemed to boil. "Maybe in detention, with me, instead of football practice?"

"No." Leonard Howard's face softened.

"Good, then leave Mr. Johnson alone." The teacher returned to her board.

Harrison tried hard to understand everything she wrote. He took notes as best he could, but his head swam with numbers and signs and letters that didn't make any sense at all. He hoped later Mrs. Kelly . . . Jennifer . . . could help him sort it all out. His mind was so jumbled that by the time the bell rang, he'd forgotten about Leonard Howard. That is, until after class.

Out in the crowded hallway, Harrison felt a finger poking his back. When he spun around, Leonard Howard was in his face.

CHAPTER SIXTEEN

HARRISON CLENCHED HIS BOOKS in one hand and a fist in the other but forced them both against his legs. "Leave me alone."

"You scared? You big retard." Howard gave Harrison a shove.

Harrison stumbled back and his head banged into a locker. He dropped his books and cocked his fist. A small crowd sprang up around them in a ring, but Becky Smart jumped between him and Leonard Howard before Harrison could let him have it.

Leonard Howard chuckled and reached over Becky's shoulder to point at Harrison. "You're lucky."

Becky swatted his hand away. "Can't you be nice?"

"You're nice enough for everybody. Another freak show for you to take care of, Little Miss Goody Two-Shoes."

"I'm not ashamed to be nice, Leo."

Leo Howard snorted.

"You play football, *Leo*?" Harrison asked, picking up his books.

"So what?" Leo stuck out his chin.

"So, I'll see you then." Harrison stared at the boy for a beat before turning and walking away.

Becky caught up with him halfway down the hall. "Where you going?"

"I got history with Mr. Guy. Room 324."

"Me too," she said. "I'll walk with you. You did good. He's such a jerk."

They climbed the stairs and Harrison said, "Coach warned me."

"About Leo?"

"About someone. He's smart, Coach."

"He's good friends with my dad."

"He said I've got to save up the anger."

"Are there other things you're angry about?"

Harrison glanced at her and touched his bad eye. "This."

"Someone did that to you?"

He nodded.

"I'm sorry," she said. "That would make anyone mad."

"There's worse things than this, believe me." Harrison stopped in front of room 324.

"That's scary," she said.

"You're right." Harrison walked into the classroom

and found an empty seat.

The first two classes were the only ones he had with Becky, but the day got better as it went on anyway because none of the other teachers were as strict as Mrs. Zebolt. Coach treated Harrison just like everyone else, and he didn't even mention that Harrison was his foster son when he introduced him as the new boy to his class. That seemed strange, but there was so much to learn and think about—including the playbook he studied during lunch—so it got lost in the chaos of the day.

Before he knew it, Harrison was weighted down with homework and standing in the boys' locker room surrounded by the noise of forty kids chattering as they dressed for football practice.

"Harrison," Coach said, appearing from nowhere and brushing right on past him, "come with me."

Harrison followed Coach down a dim hall and into a storage room, where he began rummaging around in some piles of dusty old football equipment. Piece by piece, Coach handed Harrison the pads, pants, helmet, and jersey he'd need to play.

"Um, Coach?" Harrison wiggled into a pair of rib pads to see if they fit. "Are you going to tell the team about me?"

"What do you mean?"

"That I'm . . ."

Coach raised his eyebrows. "With me?"

CHAPTER SEVENTEEN

HARRISON NODDED AT COACH.

"No," Coach said. "They'll find out when they find out. I don't tell my players anything they don't need to know. That okay with you?"

"Sure, Coach."

Coach had him try on three helmets before they found one big enough to fit, then they returned to the locker room and Coach gave him a lock. Harrison found an empty locker just about the time the rest of the kids were finishing up getting dressed and heading out to the field. Harrison's new teammates couldn't keep from glancing his way and some stared at him without trying to hide their hostility.

"I got you these during my lunch break." Coach laid a slightly used pair of football cleats on the bench.

"Thanks."

"Don't worry," Coach said. "Got your mouthpiece?"

Harrison removed the plastic mouthpiece from his pocket. Coach took it and fastened it to the metal face mask on the helmet.

"Make sure you put that in your mouth and don't take it out," Coach said. "Technically, you're not supposed to be in full pads for five days, but since I'm your guardian and your coach, it'll be fine. You won't need the rib pads; they'll take too long to lace up. Get geared up as fast as you can and meet us out there. Just walk straight out, past the tennis courts and down the hill. You'll see the varsity and the JVs on the first two fields. We'll be on the farthest one."

Coach swung open the locker room door. Sunlight spilled inside and Coach stopped short. "Harrison?"

"Yes, Coach?"

"You've never played football before. It's not easy to break onto a team once the season has already started. If you're good, the other kids will worry about you taking their jobs. If you're not good, they won't want you around. Just do your best."

CHAPTER EIGHTEEN

HARRISON MATCHED THE DIFFERENT-SHAPED pads with the pockets lining the pants and stuffed them inside. He pulled on the pants, slipped on the cleats, and slung the shoulder pads over his head. It was a struggle to pull the dark-blue practice jersey over the thick shoulder pads, but finally he was ready. The cleats clacked against the tile floor, making a lonely sound that echoed off the metal lockers.

On the way out, Harrison stopped to use the bathroom. As he washed his hands, he looked in the mirror. His bad eye looked horrible, still red where it should be white, all set in a sea of fading purple and yellow skin. He had to admit to himself that he was like a walking, talking zombie. Maybe that wouldn't matter on the football field. He'd always thought of the football field as a place where nothing else mattered, only what you are and what you can do. Butterflies swirled in his stomach. He strapped his helmet on, bit down on the mouthpiece, and headed out the door.

Yells, grunts, and the crack of pads from the varsity and JV practice fields warmed Harrison's blood. He couldn't wait.

The junior high team was spread out in orderly rows, stretching their legs. As Harrison approached, one boy pointed at him and said something to the player next to him. Word spread quickly and soon everyone was looking at him and pointing, and some of the kids were laughing out loud. Coach marched into their midst.

"That's enough chatter!"

Everyone went silent. Harrison reached the sideline and stopped.

"But Coach," one brave soul shouted, "look at him!"

All eyes were on Harrison, even Coach's. Some of the boys snickered despite Coach's glare. Harrison looked down at himself, knowing that he'd done something ridiculous and embarrassing but having no idea what.

"Harrison," Coach said, shaking his head, "come here, will you?"

CHAPTER NINETEEN

"YOU CLOWNS GET BACK to your stretching!" Coach barked at the rest of the team and they reacted right away.

"Here," Coach said, reaching for Harrison's jersey, "let's get that off of you."

"My jersey? What's wrong?" Harrison stood, limp.

"Nothing with your jersey." Coach set his clipboard down in the grass and spoke in a low voice that the rest of the team couldn't hear. "We've got to take it off so we can fix your shoulder pads."

"What's wrong with them?" Harrison lowered his voice to a whisper and shifted the uncomfortable pads on his shoulders.

Coach tried not to smile but couldn't help himself. "They're backward, Harrison. I have to admit, I thought I'd seen everything."

As Coach yanked the jersey over Harrison's head, his cheeks felt like they had a sudden sunburn. "Oh, stupid," Harrison said.

"No, not stupid." Coach unsnapped the straps and turned the pads around on Harrison's neck without taking them off. "Just funny. Don't worry about it. It's what you do with them that counts."

Coach helped get the jersey back on and slapped Harrison's shoulder pad. "Get to work."

Harrison got into a spot at the back of one of the lines on the fifty-yard line and did his best to follow the lead of the kid next to him.

"Hey." The boy reached across the space between them. "I'm Justin. Glad you got your pads on right."

Harrison studied the boy's face for a moment, saw nothing mean, and took his hand. "Harrison."

"You're big."

Harrison didn't know how to respond to that, so he kept quiet.

"Lineman, huh?" Justin said. "I'm a receiver."

Justin was small and thin, with blue eyes and dirty blond hair long enough to sprout from the edges of his helmet. Harrison hoped Justin was fast, because given his size, that was probably the only way he'd be much of a football player. Harrison wanted to think that the first friend he had—or might have—would be a good player.

"I think maybe I'm going to be a running back," Harrison said.

"You? You're a monster."

Harrison scowled and touched the skin around his eye through his face mask. "This will heal."

"No, I didn't mean a monster because of your eye." Justin laughed in a friendly way. "I meant, you're *huge*, a monster."

"Oh." Harrison felt better. "Brandon Jacobs is the Giants' running back. He's six-foot-four and two hundred and sixty pounds."

Justin blinked and nodded. "Yeah, I guess."

Stretching ended. The players formed several lines and began running through agility drills. Then Coach blew his whistle, shouting for the linemen to go with Coach Lee and the backs and receivers to join him and another assistant under the goal post. Harrison was already sweating from the agility drills and all the padding, and his helmet felt strange and uncomfortable. On the next whistle, linemen went to one part of the field while skill players—runners, receivers, quarterbacks, and defensive backs—went to another. Harrison fell in with the skill players, standing in the back of the group so he could watch and learn.

They started with a tackling drill. Coach arranged six foam half-round bags end to end in two parallel lines to create a space in the grass only about two yards wide. The players separated into two groups—one side would run the ball while the other would try to tackle that runner. All the action was to take place in the strip of grass between the bags. Harrison ended up in the tackling line. He watched as the first pair squared off, smashing into each other, with both going down. The next runner lowered a shoulder and blasted the tackler sideways, where he tripped and fell over one of the bags. The boys all cheered.

The next tackler got the best of his runner, hitting him low and upending him like a kicked bucket. More cheers.

Before he knew it, Harrison was up and, staring at him from the other end of the bags, was Leo Howard. In the embarrassment of walking out with his shoulder pads backward, Harrison had forgotten about his math class tormenter. Leo Howard's puffy lips curled into a smile around his mouthpiece. Harrison heard the boy snarl as he grabbed the ball.

The whistle blew.

Before Harrison could react, Leo Howard bolted toward him like a branded bull.

CHAPTER TWENTY

HARRISON WASN'T AFRAID, JUST unsure.

Then something snapped inside him and he took off, running right at Leo with his arms wide to make the tackle. Leo lowered his shoulder and exploded up into Harrison as if he really was a bull goring a matador with his horn. The wind left Harrison's body in a fierce gush. The earth flipped. He crashed down and saw a burst of stars. Coach blew his whistle.

Some of the kids laughed. Leo Howard strutted at the other end of the bags and tossed the ball underhand to Coach.

"Nice hit, Leo." Coach didn't even look at Harrison. "Let's go, next!"

Harrison got out of the way and switched sides like everyone before him, standing now at the back of the running backs' line. The way Coach acted hurt Harrison, but it also made him mad. He studied the players in front of him, what the runners did and the tacklers, too. He knew without anyone telling him what he'd done wrong. He was too high. The kids who got underneath their opponents, whether they were the runner or the tackler, seemed to do much better than the kids who stood up straight when they hit.

Harrison envisioned himself getting the ball and lowering his own pads. He knew he could do it. He moved steadily up in the line. Coach didn't say much to any of the kids; he just blew the whistle and watched them hit. When Harrison was next to go, he saw Leo move up two spots and cut the line so that he'd have another shot at Harrison.

Harrison sunk his teeth into his mouth guard. A growl gurgled up from his throat. What he really wanted to do was run right over, rip Leo's helmet off, and punch him in the face. He knew he couldn't, though, and instead, he breathed short huffs of breath and focused on what he would do when he had the ball.

The whistle blew—his turn.

Coach looked at him and gave him a nod so small that no one else would notice, then tossed Harrison the ball. Harrison caught it, lowered his hips, and staggered his feet to get a good running start. Leo Howard stood at the far end of the bags. He slapped his helmet once with each hand, snorted, and lowered his own stance.

The whistle blew again.

Harrison took off. Leo Howard surged toward him. Harrison felt thirteen years of hatred boiling in his brain. Leo came at him low, moving with the skill and ease of a cat. An instant before impact, Harrison lowered his shoulder, aiming it for Leo's helmet.

When they crashed together, their pads popped like a gunshot.

Harrison saw more stars.

A roar burst from his throat.

CHAPTER TWENTY-ONE

"AHHH!" HARRISON PLOWED STRAIGHT through Leo Howard.

Leo reeled sideways, tripped over the bags, and fell to the ground.

Harrison ran the length of the bags, turned, and headed back for Leo again.

He heard Coach's yell behind him. "Harrison!"

As Leo got to his feet, Harrison lowered his shoulder again, blasting Leo Howard from the side and knocking him to the ground once more.

"Harrison, no!" Coach was on him, holding him and flinging him away from the fallen player as he blew on his whistle. "It's over!"

The rest of the team looked at him wide-eyed. The red mist that had clouded Harrison's mind began to clear.

"You did good," Coach said, patting him on the shoulder, "but you only get one hit. When you hear the whistle, that's it. You understand? You can't hit anyone after the whistle. That's the game."

Coach turned on the rest of the team. "What are you all looking at? Let's go, next two up!"

Coach marched past Leo without concern, even though the red-headed boy wobbled as he got to his feet. Harrison jogged to the back of the tackling line now.

Justin fell in beside him and whispered, "Nice hit. You're a maniac. That's the first time I've ever seen anyone run Leo over. Trust me, Coach loves that stuff. He's old school."

Harrison knew what that meant, that Coach did things the way they used to be done in a time from the past, when the game was even tougher and more brutal than it was now. Part of that was having no pity for players who got stomped by their opponents. It made Harrison feel better about the way Coach ignored him after Leo knocked him down. It wasn't anything personal; that's just the way Coach was, old school.

Now it was time for Harrison to figure out the tackling side of things. He noticed that the players who did it best not only got their pads low, but they wrapped their arms and exploded up through the runner. Harrison didn't know if that was something he could do, but he had an idea how it might work. When his turn came, he smiled to himself to see that Leo hadn't cut the line to match up with him again.

Harrison got ready, burst forward at the whistle, then launched himself at the runner halfway through the bags. While he did make the tackle, he hit the runner too low and the runner was able to fall forward over the top of him to gain an extra yard.

Coach tooted his whistle. "Not bad. Knock him back next time. Drive up through him."

Harrison went to the end of the running backs' line. When Leo took his next turn, he seemed to have lost some steam. One of the other players brought him down without too much of a struggle. When Harrison was up again, he faced a solid-looking kid the others called "Bull," which was short for Bulkowski. Like about half the team, Mike Bulkowski was a ninth grader. Harrison didn't feel quite the same rage as he had against Leo. He kept his pads low, but without the intensity Bull was able to drag him down.

"On again, off again," Coach barked without looking directly at Harrison. "There's no such thing as a part-time champion. You play how you practice, boys. If you take a vacation, even for a single play in practice, you'll do the same thing in a game, and we can't win that way."

Harrison felt his ears burning again. The last thing he wanted to do was disappoint the man who was not only his coach but someone who—if he did well enough—might keep him around. He made another tackle, better than the first, but nothing that got any response from Coach. The next time he tackled, though, Harrison reminded himself of Coach's burning words, and it was like lighting a blowtorch in his brain.

Adam Varnett—another ninth grader and the team's starting halfback—took the ball and bolted forward at the whistle. Harrison ran straight for him, lowering his head, determined to get under the runner's pads. Varnett was built like a bowling bowl, short and thick, so his pads were low to start out with, and he dipped even lower at the last instant. Harrison went lower, diving and exploding up through the runner.

Varnett's knee struck the top of Harrison's helmet.

Harrison felt a stab of pain, then his neck went numb.

CHAPTER TWENTY-TWO

HARRISON STARED UP AT the sky, so pure and blue that the jet streams crisscrossed it like slash marks he'd seen kids make with chalk on the school sidewalks, marking off grids for tic-tac-toe. He heard a voice and blinked. It was Coach, but it sounded like he was at the other end of a long tunnel.

"Harrison? Are you okay?"

Harrison flexed his fingers and toes. "Did I make the tackle?"

Coach's short laugh echoed down the tunnel. "Stopped him cold. You okay?"

Harrison tried to sit up.

"You can't hit with the top of your head like that." Coach unsnapped Harrison's helmet and slipped it off his head. "Here, look at me. I need to see your eyes and make sure you didn't get a concussion."

"It looks easy on TV—you just run around and knock people over." Harrison rubbed the back of his neck. "I'm okay."

Coach turned and tooted his whistle. "Coach Lee, get them going on inside run. I got him."

Harrison saw Varnett limping away toward the next drill with the rest of the kids.

"Is Varnett okay?"

"He'll be fine. That's what knee pads are for. It was a great hit, but just don't drop your head. You gotta keep your head up when you tackle. You can break your neck, especially on special teams, like a kickoff, when you've got a running start and you slam into someone."

"I think my neck's okay."

"Your eyes are fine. You're okay, but let's get you a haircut after practice."

Harrison ran his hand through the mess of sweaty hair on top of his head. "My hair?"

"I think your helmet will fit better if we cut it short."

"Like yours?"

"If you want."

"Mrs. Constable used to cut our hair. She said if we kept it long we didn't need a hat in the winter."

"Well, Jennifer and I have plenty of extra hats."

Harrison smiled.

"All set?" Coach asked.

"I'm fine," Harrison said.

"Put your helmet back on then, and let's go."

Harrison jogged beside Coach, strapping on his

helmet. Coach ignored him when they got to the next drill, treating him like all the other kids, but Harrison felt warm on the inside when he recalled the image of Coach stepping outside himself to be nice when he thought Harrison had been hurt. Mrs. Godfrey was right.

Harrison watched Varnett and the other running back, Alan Simpson, take turns playing the position during the inside run drill. They'd huddle up with the quarterback and the offensive line, listen to the play, then line up, burst forward at the snap, take the handoff, and run. On another part of the field, wide receivers and defensive backs worked on the passing game. There were no passes in the drill they called "inside run." Players on both sides knew the focus was run blocking, run defense, tackling, and tough running by the backs. After watching for a handful of plays, Harrison asked Coach if he could try.

"Sure," Coach said in his gruff voice. "Work right into the rotation. You don't need an invitation."

After the next play, Harrison stepped into the huddle beside the quarterback. Varnett said, "This is my spot, rookie."

Harrison didn't move. He figured if Coach said he could have a turn, then he'd have it. Varnett tried to shove Harrison out of the way. Harrison turned and blasted him in the chest, knocking him backward so that he staggered into the group of players waiting for a turn. Varnett looked at Harrison with wide eyes.

"Coach told me to go in." Harrison turned back into the huddle without worrying about whether Varnett was going to come after him. Something told Harrison it would work out just fine.

Coach barked the play as if nothing had happened. "Twenty-four lead."

Harrison knew from the playbook, and from watching and listening, that a "twenty-four lead" meant that the halfback—twenty—would get the ball and run it through the four hole—between the right guard and the right tackle—and that "lead" meant that after he took the handoff, he'd follow the fullback and run through the hole. The quarterback repeated the play and they broke the huddle. Harrison lined up behind Bulkowski, the fullback. Butterflies came to life in his stomach again. This would be his first real play and it felt hugely important.

The quarterback shouted the cadence. "Blue fifty-seven, blue fifty-seven, set, hike!"

Everyone took off, including Harrison. He followed the fullback, heading for the four hole. The quarterback extended the ball into Harrison's stomach. Harrison panicked. The defensive linemen were shooting through the gaps like the offensive line was a leaky bucket.

The ball dribbled to the ground, a disaster.

Shouts filled the air.

"Fumble!"

CHAPTER TWENTY-THREE

HARRISON DIDN'T THINK. HE just scooped up the ball and held it tight.

CRASH!

Someone blasted him from the side. Harrison spun and churned his legs, driving forward, hungry to at least get the ball back to the line of scrimmage so the broken play wouldn't be a complete disaster. Another defensive player came at him. Harrison dipped his shoulder and exploded up, knocking him back. Harrison saw an opening in the line. He drove toward it, pumping his legs.

A linebacker met him in the hole. They smashed into each other and Harrison spun again, keeping his balance and finding himself suddenly in some open space. He took off into the heart of the defense. Another lineman threw his arms around Harrison's legs from behind. Harrison staggered, but his legs seemed to be working on their own and kept right on chugging. He broke free and accelerated, opening the gap between him and the biggest defenders.

There was only a single safety left and when Harrison saw him, he didn't try to run away but instead headed right for him, lowering his shoulder pad like a weapon and blasting through the safety, knocking him out of the way like he was a barn fly. Harrison heard the whistle, but he just kept running, all the way to the end zone, where he spiked the ball, bouncing it off the grass so that it flew through the air. He turned around with his fists raised to the sky.

"Touchdown!"

"Harrison!" Coach marched toward him, his face red as a fire engine. "You do that again, you're off this team! Take five laps around the field, and you better make them *fast*!"

Coach pointed toward the far end of the field. Everyone stared.

Harrison had no idea what had happened. His mouth sagged open and a small, confused noise gurgled up from his throat.

"Go!" Coach stabbed his finger in the air again.

Harrison started to run.

CHAPTER TWENTY-FOUR

HARRISON HEARD THE TWEET of Coach's whistle and the inside run continued without him. A single hot tear streaked past Harrison's nose. He ground his teeth so hard his jaw ached, but he sniffed and blinked his eyes dry.

He ran fast, like Coach said. He ran until his lungs burned and his legs went numb, and as he ran, he scolded himself. He scolded himself for ever believing people could be nice to him, or things could ever make sense, or that he could ever fit in. He was alone in the world, and that's all he'd ever be. He wasn't going to be fooled by Mrs. Godfrey's soft voice, or Jennifer's kind words, or Becky's friendly smile, or Coach taking him fishing and promising a haircut. He was going to be smarter than that. Those things were all window dressing. They weren't real, and at the end of the day, all he could really expect from people was meanness and anger and insults.

What he wanted to do was run right off the field, off school grounds, through the village, out of town, out of the state, out of the entire country. He wanted to run to Canada and start a new life, maybe living on the street. That's how crazy his mind was, but in the end, he finished his five laps and stood gasping for breath, ready for more cruelty and punishment. The team kept doing inside run, but no one said anything to Harrison, and he ignored them right back. He just stood there, off to the side, watching but not participating.

Coach acted like he wasn't there until he blew his whistle and shouted, "Good work. Get a drink."

The team rushed for a water spigot that stood off on the edge of their field, closer to the JV field. A pipe stuck out of the ground with a faucet someone turned on so that streams of water burst from a long plastic pipe suspended chest-high by legs on either end. Harrison watched the team lining up behind one another like cows at the trough. He didn't notice that Coach was beside him until he spoke in his gruff voice.

"Harrison, why in the world did you do that?"

Harrison's face twisted with rage and confusion. "I don't even know what you're talking about."

CHAPTER TWENTY-FIVE

COACH STARED HARD AT him for a moment. "Really?"

Harrison shook his head. "I thought I was supposed to run them over. I know I messed up on the handoff, but I did the best I could to get the ball back and try to gain some yards."

"I know that," Coach said, "that was incredible. That wasn't the problem."

Harrison looked at Coach in total confusion.

"You can't spike the ball, don't you know that?" Coach asked.

"No," Harrison said.

"Are you for real?"

Harrison shrugged and sputtered. "I guess so. That's what they do on TV."

Coach shook his head. "This is junior high school

football. Spiking the ball is a fifteen-yard penalty. It's unsportsmanlike. It makes your whole team look bad, your school, and especially your coach. I don't let anybody do that. Sportsmanship is first with me. I cut a kid last year for spitting on someone after he made a tackle. I just won't have it. It's more important than winning and losing. It's a life lesson that goes way beyond football. Do you understand?"

Harrison tried to understand. Finally he said, "I don't, Coach. I'm sorry. I'm just being honest. I don't see how it's okay they do that in the NFL but it's wrong here."

Coach glanced impatiently at the team. Some of the boys were finished drinking and headed back toward Coach, strapping up their helmets as they jogged.

"Can we talk about it later?" Coach asked.

"Sure."

"And in the meantime, can you promise me you won't do that again?" Coach asked.

"I won't do it."

"Good. Can you run like that again?"

Harrison smiled big. "That's all I want to do."

"Good. We're going to do some team work now. I'm going to have Coach Lee work with you off to the side on taking a handoff. You watch for a few plays, then when I give you the nod, you get in there. Also, I liked the way you shoved Varnett right back when he tried to take your spot in the huddle."

"That was good?" Harrison asked, his forehead wrinkling up under his helmet. "That wasn't unsportsmanlike?"

"No, that was just standing your ground and being tough," Coach said. "That was good."

"Coach, you're making my head spin."

"Relax. You'll get it, and when you do, Harrison, I think you could be great. But that was just one run. Maybe you were just lucky."

Coach gave his whistle a blast. "Let's find out."

CHAPTER TWENTY-SIX

HARRISON HAD NEVER BEFORE felt so much joy for such a long period of time, and when they lined up and ran sprints and Coach called them in to wrap up practice, Harrison didn't want it to end. There were a couple times where two defenders got onto his legs at the same time and then another one or two players were able to topple him over, but otherwise, every time he touched the football, Harrison sprinted, blasted, spun, and plowed his way into the end zone. He was bigger and faster than everyone. He was like a man among boys.

It was more than just his size, speed, and strength. It was his intensity—even Coach said so. There was a well of fiery red anger inside him that he could just tap into when he had the ball in his hands. It would erupt out of him, and then he could just cap it until the next time he had the chance to hit within the rules of the game. It was magical, and it left him calm and tired and happy.

During the course of practice, Harrison had sent three kids to the sideline with bumps and bruises. One of them was Leo Howard. In fact, Harrison had looked for Leo during the mayhem of each play. If Leo was even close to being between Harrison and the goal line, Harrison attacked him. Harrison wasn't sure if he really did hurt Leo's shoulder or if Leo faked it just to avoid Harrison's repeated punishment. Either way, the big red-headed linebacker couldn't even look at Harrison as the team buzzed about in the locker room changing into their street clothes.

The only thing that felt better to Harrison than taming Leo Howard were the words he heard Coach Lee say to Coach during practice. After a thirty-yard run into the end zone that had Harrison leaping over two tacklers and dragging three more across the goal line on his back, the coaches told Harrison to take a couple plays off. He stood huffing behind the huddle when Coach Lee leaned close to Coach and whispered in a voice loud enough for Harrison to just make out, "That kid is *unstoppable*."

Coach glanced at his assistant. "Harrison? I know. I just wish he could play this week. We've got to get this one. Then next week, *with* him? This whole team will be unstoppable."

"And you'll get the varsity job."

Coach grinned. "I know no one does this for the money, but it'll be a nice pay raise for us both. I've had my eye on a new fishing boat."

Harrison banged his locker shut and swelled with pride as he remembered the coaches' words and that *he*, Harrison Johnson, would be able to bring such good fortune not only to the entire team but to his new family.

"Hey." Justin jabbed Harrison's shoulder. "Like I said, a monster."

Harrison blushed. "It was fun."

"Fun for you. The rest of us need three days off. Do you live in the village?"

"Yes."

"Good. You want to get some Subway?"

"Subway?"

"A sandwich. A lot of us go after practice on our way home. We're supposed to keep our weight up, you know."

"No. Thanks, though." Harrison didn't have any money, but he didn't want to say that was the reason.

"Aw, come on. My treat. I cut three lawns on Sunday and the cash is burning a hole in my pocket."

"You get money for cutting lawns?" The idea of work wasn't strange to Harrison, but getting paid for his efforts had been unthinkable.

"Sure, a lot. People in the village like their lawns cut. Twice a week, some of them."

"Could I do that?"

"I can help you find some work, sure."

"So I'll let you buy me a sub," Harrison said, "but only if you promise I can cut a lawn to pay you back."

Justin laughed. "You don't have to do that."

"Yes, I do."

Justin shrugged. "Sure, you can cut one for me. We can go into business together."

"Hang on, will you?" Harrison left his new friend and found Coach in his office.

After knocking, Harrison went inside and closed the door behind him. Two metal lockers stood in the corner by a private bathroom. The scent of mold crept into Harrison's nose. Coach sat at a desk facing the wall, drawing up plays.

"Sorry about hurting those guys," Harrison said.

Coach's serious face broke into a grin. "That's part of the game. They're all fine. This team needs to be tougher, is the problem. Don't you worry about it."

Harrison stuffed his hands in his pockets. "Can I go to Subway and get my hair cut later? Justin's going to pay, but I said only if he lets me cut one of his lawns to pay him back. He said I can go into business with him. Can I do that? Can I work and make money, or do you need me to work at the house?"

Coach tilted back in his chair and thumbed his hat back on his head so the brim stood up almost straight. "Work at the house?"

Harrison shrugged. "You want me to work, right?"

"You can help out a little, I guess. Take out the trash.

Maybe cut the grass, but I'd pay you for that."

Harrison narrowed his eyes. "You'd pay *me*? Why?"

"That's what families do. When kids help out around the house, they get paid for it. Not everything, but jobs like that, the grass, shoveling the driveway, digging a ditch."

"You don't have to do that," Harrison said. "You feed me, I need to work."

Coach sat up and put a hand on Harrison's shoulder. "Everyone under our roof gets fed. That's not a big deal. Trust me."

"So is Subway okay?"

"Sure. Tell you what—I'll head over to the phone store and get you a cell phone, then I'll pick you up at Subway and we'll go get the haircut. Lots to do before six-thirty. Jennifer likes to eat right at six-thirty."

Harrison nodded because Mrs. Constable put the food on the table at the exact same time every night as well. "Did you say a cell phone?"

Coach leaned back in his chair again and it squealed in pain. "So we can keep in touch. Most of the kids seem to have them. That all right?"

Harrison felt a rush of excitement. "I'd love a cell phone."

"I'll get you the basic plan," Coach said. "If you want to use it more and text all the time like the rest of these characters, you can pay for that with your lawn money. Deal?"

"Sure, Coach. Thanks." Harrison turned to go but

stopped halfway out the door at the sound of Coach's voice.

"And Harrison?"

"Yes?"

"That was some performance out there today. You're one heck of a runner."

"Thanks, Coach."

Harrison hurried back into the locker room but slowed down when he saw Justin standing in the middle of a small group that included Varnett, Bulkowski, and Leo Howard. When Leo saw Harrison, he poked a finger in Justin's chest, said something, then faded out the door with his buddies, leaving Justin alone in the corner.

"What was that about?" Harrison asked, scowling at the door.

Justin's face was pale. He swallowed and nodded in the direction Leo and his buddies had gone. "He is such a rat, and now he's got it in for you big time. His dad's some lawyer in the district attorney's office and, I swear, he thinks he rules the world."

"What's that got to do with me?"

"I'm not sure," Justin said, "but he said when his dad gets done, you won't be playing on this team after tomorrow."

CHAPTER TWENTY-SEVEN

"CAN HE DO THAT?" Harrison asked.

"Of course not," Justin said, slamming his locker shut. "He just likes to talk big. Ignore him. The guy's been smelling too many of his own farts."

They laughed together at that and Harrison followed Justin out of the locker room, across the school yard, and down the sidewalk into the center of town, where a handful of teammates waited for them outside the Subway. They all went inside, ordered their subs and sodas, and sat down together to eat.

Harrison didn't say much, but he could tell by the way the other boys looked at him that they admired what he'd done on the practice field.

"So much for Varnett," a boy named Scott Rutledge said before stuffing the last piece of sub into his mouth.

"I hope he enjoys his last game as the starting halfback."

Harrison focused his eyes on his bag of chips, thinking of Leo Howard's words to Justin, even though Justin had told him to ignore the whole thing.

Justin patted him on the back. "You must have been a terror in Pop Warner. Where'd you play?"

"I didn't," Harrison said.

"Sure, you just went out there today and ran through the rest of us like a snowplow on a crowded street and it was the first time you carried the football."

"It was."

Everyone got quiet. There were six of them sitting in the long booth. Harrison was on the end.

"You're serious!" Justin said. "Holy moly, can I be your agent?"

Everyone laughed.

"That's why we've got to beat East Manfield," Scott said. "After that, we'll have the big man here in the backfield and then we can win *everything*."

"I don't think Brookton won a junior high championship in the last ten years, did we?" Justin asked.

"How could anyone in this region win with Black Creek? Those guys are all like Harrison," Scott said.

"Black Creek?" Harrison hadn't heard mention of the school.

"Their junior high team has its *own* turf field. You believe that? These guys live in the weight room from fifth grade on. Their coach is a maniac."

"He makes Coach Kelly look like a school nurse," Rutledge said.

Everyone laughed.

"Now, if we beat East Manfield—which, how could we not?" Rutledge shrugged. "And, if we get Harrison rolling, even Black Creek can't hang with us. As long as Leo Howard is full of cat crap—which he usually is—then I'm going to make some space on my dresser for that championship trophy tonight."

"What about Leo?" Harrison asked, glancing at Justin.

Rutledge took a gulp of soda and waved his hand in the air. "Cat crap. He said something like you're not eligible to play."

"How could I not be eligible?" Harrison asked.

"Exactly my point," Rutledge said.

"His dad's with the D.A.," one of the other boys said.

"So what?" Justin said. "He's gonna plant drugs in Harrison's locker? Or, like, Harrison's got some kind of criminal record? Like he's some murderer. Hey, who'd you kill, Harrison?"

The boys all grinned at him, chuckling at the silly joke.

"Harrison?"

CHAPTER TWENTY-EIGHT

HARRISON'S GUT CHURNED AND he choked back the stomach acid in his throat. "You guys are crazy."

They all laughed out loud.

"You should see your face!" Justin howled.

The joy from the friendship and the football field drained out of Harrison. "My last foster father died. It was an accident. On the farm. I saw it happen."

The silence at the table got even bigger when the woman behind the register cackled with the guy making the subs after he spurted mayonnaise on his shirt.

"Sorry, Harrison." Justin spoke quietly and put a hand on Harrison's shoulder. "We were just goofing."

"I know." Harrison stood. "It's okay. I'll see you guys tomorrow."

As he walked away, no one spoke. He stepped outside

and saw Coach's truck pulling into the parking lot. Harrison crossed the pavement and climbed in. Coach put the truck in gear and off they went.

"How was Subway?" Coach asked, turning the corner and heading up Main Street. "I hope you didn't ruin your dinner."

"Fine."

"Look, here's that phone. I put my number and Jennifer's in it for you already so you can call us if you want."

Harrison took the phone, something he should have been thrilled with but could only hold quietly.

Coach took a closer look at him. "I thought you'd love a phone."

"No, I do, Coach. It's great."

"What's wrong?"

Harrison stared straight ahead at the traffic. "I told them, the guys."

"That you're our foster child? That's okay. I wasn't trying to hide it; I just wanted it to come out naturally, and now it did."

"Not that. I told them about Mr. Constable—*not* that I killed him but that it was an accident."

"Of course you didn't kill him, Harrison." Coach pulled the truck over. "We all know what happened. Why would that even come up?"

The words gushed out of Harrison's mouth. "They were kidding. They didn't know, but someone said it as a joke. Leo Howard's dad is with the D.A. and Leo is telling people I won't be here after tomorrow. Then someone joked that I must have been a criminal and I just told them. Can he do that? Stop me from playing?"

"Leo Howard's dad?" Coach's face went from angry to confused to worried. "Oh boy."

CHAPTER TWENTY-NINE

"OH BOY, WHAT?" HARRISON asked.

Coach set his jaw and pulled the truck back out into traffic. "Let's get your hair cut. Don't worry about Leo Howard, or his father. I'll handle them."

"But you said, 'oh boy.' Why did you say that?"

"He's just . . ." Coach swatted the air next to his head. "He's a pain in the *neck*, and this is not what I need right now, but don't worry. I've done battle with people worse than him."

Harrison thought about the picture of Coach in his Army uniform, ready for action in the desert. "You mean in the war?"

"That's not really what I meant, but I guess that fits."

"And they were trying to kill you."

"Yes, they were."

"And Leo Howard's father's not that bad."

"Maybe not." Coach turned the truck into the parking lot of a small strip of shops.

Harrison followed him inside the salon. The bell jingled and the smell of chemicals and hairspray hit him like a wave.

"Hi, Denise," Coach said to a heavyset woman who was dusting hair off a black vinyl barber's chair.

"I'm ready for you." She patted the chair.

"Not me, him." Coach pointed a thumb at Harrison.

"Oh, great. What are we doing?"

"Just cut it real short so my helmet fits," Harrison said.

Denise patted the chair again. "Right here. Your helmet? You got a new football player, Coach? That's some shiner he's got."

"Denise, this is Harrison. He's our foster son, and it so happens that he *is* a pretty good football player."

Harrison tried not to glow.

Denise cut his hair short, but both she and Coach figured out together that he should leave a bit more on top to give him some style to go with the close-cut sides and back. Harrison stared at himself in the mirror. He looked like an entirely different person, and not in a bad way.

"Thanks," Harrison said to Coach, uncomfortable at the sight of him opening up his wallet.

"You're very welcome," Coach said, taking the change and giving back a couple bills to Denise as a tip.

In the truck, Coach said, "You look good."

Harrison couldn't stop running his fingers across the soft stubble. When Jennifer saw him, she gave a low whistle and said, "Handsome." That made Harrison blush maybe harder than he ever had before, but partly because when she said it, Harrison immediately thought of Becky Smart.

After dinner, Jennifer removed an apple pie from the oven and put it out on the table along with a half-gallon of vanilla ice cream. Harrison had never tasted anything so sweet and delicious, and Jennifer served him three portions before he finally could eat no more. Harrison did his homework at the kitchen table. Jennifer sat next to him and helped before they joined Coach in the other room. In the warm light of the living room, as darkness gathered outside and the three of them sat slowly flipping pages of their books, Harrison thought he might be in heaven. The good food and the long, hard practice left his eyes heavy and fluttering.

"How about bed?" Coach said a little after nine. "You'll be sore in the morning."

Harrison went to bed and lay there listening to the garbled sound of his new foster parents talking at the other end of the hall behind closed doors. When the nasty memory of Leo Howard and the look of concern on Coach's face came to roost in his mind, Harrison was thankful to be too tired to pay them much notice. Instead, he turned on his side and went to sleep.

In the morning, Harrison was sore. His whole body ached, but nothing more than his neck. He crawled out of bed, got ready for school, and hobbled downstairs into the smell of coffee and eggs crackling in their pan. Coach put down the paper and looked at his watch. "You're moving slow. Don't worry, you'll feel better once the blood gets flowing."

Coach's cell phone buzzed. He looked at the number and scowled before he even answered it. "This is Coach Kelly . . . Yes, Mark. How can I help you? . . . I guess I can do that. My lunch break is at eleven forty-five. I can meet you in my office by the gym. . . . Fine, I'll see you then."

"What was that about?" Jennifer asked.

Coach frowned. "Leo Howard's dad wants to meet."

Harrison sat at his place and drank some orange juice, eager for the eggs Jennifer was sliding out of the pan and onto his plate. "Is that about me, Coach?"

Jennifer froze, and a fried egg hung on the lip of the pan before dropping onto Coach's plate.

"What does Leo Howard's dad have to do with Harrison?" she asked.

Coach set down the paper and picked up his fork. "Nothing."

"It's never nothing with that man, Ron."

"Harrison bested his kid yesterday. Leo's not a bad

player, but he grew up thinking he's doing the rest of us a favor by just being around. The kids go along with it because he's bigger and better than most of them, but Harrison rocked his world a bit."

"Rocked his world? What does that mean?" Jennifer set the pan in the sink.

"Busted him in the mouth." Coach took a bite of toast.

Jennifer spun around. "Not literally? Harrison didn't get into a fight with him—he didn't punch him, did he?"

"No, just blew through him like a bulldozer. Kid bruised his shoulder, I guess. Probably hurt his pride more than anything, but with a kid like that, pride hurts more than blood and bones."

"How did you know his father was calling about you, Harrison?" Jennifer asked.

Harrison had been watching the two of them like a tennis match. Now he swallowed and said, "He told Justin Rabin that I wasn't going to be eligible after today."

"And?" Jennifer looked at Coach.

Coach finished his last bite of egg and got up from the table. "It's all hogwash."

"Why aren't you looking at me?" Jennifer asked him.

Coach stopped and turned. "What?"

"In the eye," she said.

Coach slowly raised his eyes. His shoulders slumped.

"There's something you're not telling us," she said. "What is it?"

CHAPTER THIRTY

"I'M HIS GUARDIAN *AND* his coach," Coach said, sounding like one of the lawyers Harrison had heard from time to time making their arguments in the courthouse. "So there's this rule about not having pads on for the first week of practice and I kind of glossed over that part because I want Harrison to get into the groove as fast as he can. It's a silly rule for kids who are . . . who are . . . Well, not a kid as big and strong as Harrison. He laid waste to half the team. *He* wasn't in any danger, I can promise you that."

Silence hung for a moment before Jennifer said, "But you broke the rules."

"I waived the rules. I'm his guardian, for God's sake, and his coach. These rules are made up by people who have no idea."

Jennifer sighed. "But when Mark Howard gets onto this, he'll press the issue, won't he? Of course he will. He's an obnoxious, pompous jerk."

"I can handle him," Coach said.

"Oh no. *I* can handle him, not you." Jennifer tugged off her apron, wiped her hands, and threw it down in the sink. "I'll get my briefcase and stop there on the way to my office. Don't you speak with him."

"Jennifer, I'll be fine."

She stopped and turned on him, pointing right at his face. "You've worked too hard for this, Ron Kelly. All those nights watching film in the basement? Standing in the rain scouting the other teams? Baking in the sun during two-a-day practices? Now Harrison comes to us—not because you tried to find a boy who was big and fast and strong, but because I needed a child in our home, and because he needed us. And now some fathead like Mark Howard is going to mess that up because Harrison knocked his kid over on a *football field*? I don't think so."

"I said, I can handle it."

"He'll tear you apart, Ron. You were wrong and you know it. *He'll* know it, and he'll use it to make you mad, and you'll get mad. Worst case, you punch his lights out. Best case, you scream and slam your fist and the school administrators get involved and it'll be a mess no one will be able to sort out. Let me do what I do, Ron. He might be a lawyer, but I'm a better one.

Let me fight fire with fire."

"What are you going to say?"

"That you didn't break the rules."

"But I kind of did."

"Really? Well, that all depends on how people interpret the rules, right? Now think. Was there anything, any piece of equipment at all that Harrison didn't have on yesterday? I mean, it was his first day ever. Did he leave something behind?"

"I put my shoulder pads on backwards," Harrison said, trying to be helpful.

"No." Jennifer shook her head.

Coach snapped his fingers. "Rib pads. I told him to forget his rib pads because they'd take too long to lace up, but you don't *have* to have rib pads to play."

"But he has rib pads and he didn't wear them," Jennifer said. "So I can honestly say that he wasn't in *full* pads, and I can say that you allowed him to wear some pads as a precaution. All I need is a thread, and I've got it. Trust me, Ron. You don't want anyone but me to handle this."

Coach looked at Harrison and pointed a thumb at Jennifer. "Is she smart, or what?"

Harrison grinned. He was used to lawyers using their tricks against him; he never imagined they could use the same tricks to *help* people.

"Great," Coach said. "Okay, Harrison, let's get going. My new fishing boat is still in the picture."

"Don't go buying a new boat yet," Jennifer said.

Coach stopped with his hand on the door. "You said you'd take care of it."

"I said I'd try, and I will."

"Then that's it."

"I hope that's it, but I make no guarantees," she said. "You two get to school. I'll call you and let you know how it goes."

CHAPTER THIRTY-ONE

IN MATH CLASS, LEO Howard sneered at Harrison but said nothing. Harrison could hear Leo muttering things under his breath from time to time, but he stayed busy paying attention to Mrs. Zebolt. When the teacher called on Harrison, he was ready. He stepped up to the board and finished the problem without a pause.

Mrs. Zebolt sniffed. "Not bad, Harry."

"Harrison." The name popped out of Harrison's mouth without him thinking.

"Excuse me?"

Harrison stood in front of the class feeling big and awkward and silly with his new haircut and his discolored eye. "That's my name."

"I know. Harry."

"That's not my name, Mrs. Zebolt. It's Harrison."

"Harrison. Harry. Stop looking for trouble and go back to your seat."

"Hey, Harry!" Leo Howard crooned from his seat. "Harry Johnson."

The class giggled. Mrs. Zebolt adjusted her little round glasses so that they sat crooked on her face. "Never mind that. Sit down, Harry."

Harrison stood rooted to the floor. He crossed his arms and gritted his teeth. "No."

"You'll sit down right now or you'll sit in the principal's office."

Harrison felt tears welling up in his eyes. He bit the inside of his cheek. "My name is Harrison."

"Come on, have a seat, *Harry Johnson.*" Leo Howard patted Harrison's seat.

"I told you I knew about your past and I also told you it wasn't going to be that way here. Go!" Mrs. Zebolt's face turned red. "Right now, to the office."

"Harrison," he said.

"You go, mister!"

"Call me Harrison. That's my name."

Mrs. Zebolt dug into her desk drawer and came up with a wooden ruler. "You don't tell *me*!"

The teacher raised the ruler and switched it at Harrison. He snatched the ruler instinctively and snapped it in two as easily as Leo's pencil before he chucked the pieces against the grease board. The broken ruler clattered to the floor. Mrs. Zebolt's mouth fell open before she ran to the phone on the wall, snatched it up, and shouted, "I need security in my classroom! I need the police!"

Harrison didn't move. He stood like a stage actor, looking out over an audience entranced by a magical performance, round and oval faces whose mouths and eyes strained wide in disbelief and were lit by the excitement of a mob.

In the corner, only Becky Smart looked worried.

CHAPTER THIRTY-TWO

HARRISON SAT AT THE end of the conference table. The principal, Mr. Fisk, sat at the opposite end. On one side of Harrison was the baby-faced Officer Lewin and Mr. Sofia, the guidance counselor. On the other side Coach stared down at his clenched hands. Officer Lewin was the chubby cop who gently led Harrison out of the classroom by the elbow. Once he saw the uniform, Harrison's feet came unglued from the floor.

"Coach Kelly, we just can't have Harrison disrupting classes in this way." The principal wore a sad and tired face with wrinkles built up on his forehead beneath the shiny dome of his head. Little wisps of gray hair surrounded his ears. Dark plastic frames held lenses thick enough to shrink his eyes. "I understand Harrison has had a troubled past, but this is a school, not a reformatory."

The door swung open and Jennifer slipped inside before closing it behind her. She slid a chair into place between Coach and Harrison and put a hand on Harrison's leg, giving it a good squeeze.

"I got here as fast as I could," she said.

Mr. Fisk cleared his throat and said, "I'm sorry, but I was just saying that maybe we should be looking to find a place better suited for someone with Harrison's . . . issues."

Jennifer's back stiffened. "What *issues*?"

The principal looked from Coach to the policeman for support, lowered his voice, and said, "Mrs. Kelly, we all know Harrison has a history of violence. He completely disrupted Mrs. Zebolt's math class today, and everyone's talking about what happened in football practice yesterday. I'm thinking of Harrison as much as the other students. The best thing we can do is find him another place."

CHAPTER THIRTY-THREE

"FOOTBALL PRACTICE?" JENNIFER SEEMED to have to fight to keep her voice from exploding. "Kids are supposed to be aggressive. It's football, Mr. Fisk."

"It's a symptom of the greater problem."

Jennifer turned to Harrison. Speaking in a soft voice, she asked, "What happened, Harrison?"

"In football?"

"In school today."

"He stood in front of the entire class and refused to sit down," Mr. Fisk said. "Then he snapped Mrs. Zebolt's ruler and threw it at her."

"I didn't throw it at her," Harrison said.

Jennifer turned a glare at the principal that belied the gentleness of her voice. "Mr. Fisk, I'm asking Harrison his version of what happened. That's customary in cases like this."

"Mrs. Kelly, please, this isn't a case." The principal's brow added four more lines of worry.

"Whatever you call it, I'd like to hear what my son has to say." Her words didn't leave room for anything else. "Go on, Harrison."

Harrison looked at his hands. "I did a math problem at the board. Mrs. Zebolt told me to sit down, but she called me Harry. I told her that wasn't my name, but she said she'd tell me what my name was or wasn't and then the kids started calling me 'Harry Johnson' and laughing and I just stayed where I was. I said I wasn't going to sit down until she called me Harrison. . . . That's when she took out her ruler and switched it at me."

"She *hit* you?" Jennifer's voice whirred to life like a plugged-in vacuum cleaner.

"No," Harrison said, "but I thought she was going to."

"She threatened you with it?"

Harrison nodded. "I think."

"She raised the ruler and *switched* it at you?"

"Yes." He nodded.

Jennifer looked pointedly around the room at the three men.

Mr. Fisk sputtered for a moment. "This is the first I've heard of anything like that."

"Did you bother to *ask*?" Jennifer almost came up out of her seat, and Coach's strong hand seemed to be the only thing keeping her tethered to the chair.

It was Mr. Fisk's turn to look down, and Harrison felt a small ray of hope. Up to this point he only had visions of how his whole life would come unraveled yet again.

"She tried to hit you," Jennifer said patiently to Harrison. "Then what?"

"I didn't even think about it," Harrison said. "I guess I just grabbed the ruler and broke it and I threw it. I didn't want to get hit. I didn't do anything wrong. I didn't want to do anything bad."

Officer Lewin cleared his throat. "When I got to the room, he was just standing there. He came along quietly."

Mr. Fisk shot the officer a dirty look.

"Mr. Fisk," Jennifer said, "at this point my expectation is a full investigation into the threat of physical violence your teacher made to my son. You'd be fortunate if I didn't also contact the attorney general's office to have them press charges on a hate crimes violation."

"Hate crime?" Mr. Fisk's rosy cheeks turned pale green. "This boy isn't a minority."

Jennifer raised a single eyebrow. "Obviously you haven't looked closely at his records. His maternal grandmother was a full-blooded Native American. Relax, Mr. Fisk. You're lucky my husband is part of the faculty because that makes me reluctant to turn this into more than it probably should be."

Mr. Fisk blinked and nodded. "And?"

"I want Mrs. Zebolt to apologize to Harrison, in front of the class. I then want him transferred to another math teacher. Also, all this talk about sports eligibility needs to end right now. There's a pattern of harassment here that makes me *burn*."

"Mrs. Kelly, I'm only the principal."

"Mr. Howard assured me of his cooperation this morning, if that's what you're worried about, but I want you to take care of all the other loose lips around this ship. I want your support for Harrison, and for my husband."

"Ron?" Mr. Fisk said. "You're going along with all this?"

All eyes turned to Coach.

CHAPTER THIRTY-FOUR

"IT'S BETTER NOT TO fight her, Mr. Fisk. I learned that early on," Coach said.

Mr. Fisk pinched his lips together before he spoke. "Well, I'll look into this, of course, and if Mrs. Zebolt did threaten to strike him I'll have to take action. The union will have to be involved, you know that. . . . I can't speak to the apology, Mrs. Kelly. We have to follow procedures."

"That's fine, but I want Harrison out of that class."

"Absolutely. That's in everyone's best interest."

"And I want him back at practice today. Don't even think about suspending my son until you have proof positive that he did anything but protect himself from a physical assault."

Mr. Fisk sighed deeply.

"What class do you have right now, Harrison?" she asked.

Coach looked at his watch. "My class. I had to have Miss Frank cover for me."

"Well?" Jennifer stared at the principal.

Finally he spoke. "Harrison, you can go to class while I look into this."

"And practice," Jennifer said.

"Yes, that too," the principal said. "Officer Lewin, please stay close."

"That's right," Jennifer said. "Mrs. Zebolt might need to be restrained."

"Jennifer, please." Coach stood up. "I'll take Harrison to class."

Harrison didn't think the staring and whispering could get any worse than it was his first day, but he had been wrong. He felt like the freak show at a state fair midway. Thankfully for him, Becky didn't pay the rest of the school any mind. She sat with Harrison at lunch and talked to him like nothing had happened.

Halfway through his second sandwich, Harrison said, "You sure you want to sit here with me?"

"Why wouldn't I?" Becky's eyes seemed to sparkle with mischief.

Harrison looked around, sending people's gazes scattering like schools of fish in the shadow of a shark. "Everyone's looking."

"A lot of girls spend a lot of time in front of the mirror

just hoping people will look."

"Not this kind of looking," Harrison said.

Becky reached across the lunch table and took hold of his wrist. "Let them look. I like you, Harrison. I liked the way you wouldn't sit down when that old bat wouldn't call you by your real name, and I know you're not mean or dangerous or any of that nonsense. People are always scared of something new. My dad says that if you're staying with the Kellys, that's good enough for him."

Harrison looked at her hand, afraid to touch it, and afraid to move.

"I'm sorry." She took it away.

"No, don't be sorry. That's crazy. You're, like, the nicest person I've ever met. You're like the Kellys. Did you ever meet Mrs. Kelly's mom, Mrs. Godfrey?"

"No, but Mrs. Kelly did my father's will," she said. "She's smart."

"I'm going to be a lawyer when I grow up."

"Not a fashion model?"

Becky's cheeks flushed. "My dad says women should use their brains."

"You don't think there are smart fashion models?"

"What are you going to be?"

"A football player."

Becky giggled.

"What?"

"I'm sorry. Justin Rabin told me you put your shoulder

pads on backward. I know yesterday was the first time you ever played."

"Did he tell you I ran him over like everyone else?" Harrison realized his words came out in a growl.

"Oh, don't get mad. He practically worships you. Yes, he told me what you did to everyone. I just thought it was funny that one day you're putting your shoulder pads on backward and the next day you're ready for the NFL."

"Coach says I can be great, that's all. Football is my ticket."

"I don't doubt it," she said. "Not from what everyone was saying. You know, no one listens to that jerk Leo."

"What's *he* saying?"

"That you won't even be allowed on the team after today. That's not true, is it?"

"Not from what Jennifer says."

"Jennifer?"

"Mrs. Kelly," Harrison said. "She said I could call her Mom, or Jennifer."

"What? Mom?" Becky tilted her head. "I don't get it."

Harrison looked into her deep green eyes, searching for the joke. "Coach told you I was in their family. I thought you kept it quiet from everyone just to be nice, so people wouldn't feel bad for me, being Coach's foster kid and all."

"I'm sorry, he said you were joining them, but I didn't know they were your foster parents."

Harrison looked away, then felt her hand squeeze his wrist again.

"No, don't do that. I think it's great. You're so lucky."

Harrison snuck a look at her. Her eyes were wide and honest and it made him feel much better. "I don't know about luck."

"I do. Coach and Mrs. Kelly are awesome."

"Maybe I'm lucky now, right?" Harrison's fingers strayed to the old bruise around his eye.

"For sure."

He put his hand down in his lap. "And maybe from now on, everything is going to go my way, right?"

"Sure. Maybe."

CHAPTER THIRTY-FIVE

"HARRISON, IN MY OFFICE. Okay?" Coach called to him from across the locker room.

Harrison set his helmet down on the bench and marched in.

"Listen, everything's fine, but I'm going to keep you out of the contact drills the rest of the week. Just to be safe. Oh, and don't wear your rib pads." Coach winked at him and shooed him out of the office.

For the next four days, Harrison had to stay out of contact drills, and that hurt. Worst of all was watching on Saturday when his team took the field against East Manfield. Harrison dressed in full uniform like everyone else and ran through the pregame warm-up drills, but when it came to game time, Harrison had to take a seat on the bench.

Coach put a hand on his shoulder pad and leaned over to whisper into his helmet's ear hole. "Trust me, if there was any way to let you play, I'd do it. My career is hanging on this doggone game. We should win it, though, Harrison. We really should. Then next week? Look out."

CHAPTER THIRTY-SIX

THEY DID WIN, BY two touchdowns. The team cheered and swarmed Coach, everyone reaching out just to touch him, and his face seemed to shine. When they got home after a long bus ride from East Manfield, Jennifer—who had driven to the game in her car—met Coach at the door and kissed him until Harrison blushed. They separated and both of them laughed as they each put an arm around Harrison and led him inside.

Jennifer took a roasted chicken out of the oven and pots of mashed potatoes, gravy, and steamed corn off the stove. Harrison wolfed down his food, hungry for the coming week, and eager to build his muscles and strength for the first football game of his life.

On Sunday they went to church. After a midday meal, Harrison put on some jeans and a T-shirt and met Justin at Dr. Smart's big house on the hill. Justin led him around to the back, where a lawn mower sat in the detached garage.

"You ever drive one of these?" Justin pointed to a green John Deere riding mower.

"I can drive a tractor," Harrison said. "That thing is easy."

"Okay, I'll let you do the easy part, this time." Justin pointed to a push mower in the corner. "Next time, you do the grunt work."

"I'll push today." Harrison reached for the small mower. "I owe you."

"No." Justin guided him toward the rider. "Just watch. I'll do the detail work today, everything around the edges. Trust me, it's a good payback. I'll be done with this whole job in half the time and I need that. Doc doesn't like to hear the mowers on Sunday."

Harrison looked toward the house. He was hoping he might see Becky. "Are they home?"

"No, but Doc said they'd be back at three and he asked me to be finished by then."

"Well, let's go," Harrison said.

They finished right at three and were putting the mowers away in the garage when they heard Dr. Smart's Suburban pull up in front of the house.

"Doc'll be happy." Justin wiped sweat from his forehead. "Come on."

Harrison followed Justin down the driveway, passing

the house and the circular drive in front. He glanced up, hoping to see Becky, and was surprised not only to see her but to see her walking toward them with two bottles of orange Gatorade.

"Hey, guys." She held out the bottles and smiled. "Dad said the lawn looks great and you need to stay hydrated. Here."

Justin accepted the folded money she handed him. "Thanks, Becky."

"Did you get all those math problems done, Harrison?" she asked.

"Uh, yup." Harrison hated the sound of his low, gravelly voice.

Becky smiled. "Well, see you tomorrow."

They watched her walk back up the hill. She turned and waved before disappearing into the house.

Justin stood frozen in place. "Man, she is the bomb."

"Come on." Harrison tugged Justin's sleeve. "It's not polite to stare."

On the street, Justin told him the next job would be tomorrow after dinnertime. "I already told Mrs. Peabody you'd be working with me, but I'll meet you there and show you where everything is and pay you for today. That's only because I've got to get change for these bills."

"You don't have to pay me for today. I'm working off my sub."

"Okay, I get it. Still, that was what, six bucks? You just made yourself fifteen, so I owe you nine."

"You get thirty dollars for this?"

"Doc's rolling in it. Another good reason for you to marry his daughter." Justin grinned.

Harrison put him in a loose headlock and pretended to punch him in the stomach. "Don't say that."

They both laughed.

"Man, she sure is friendly to you," Justin said.

"She's friendly to you, too," Harrison said.

"Not the same."

They got to the end of the driveway, said good-bye, and headed their separate ways.

Back home, Coach was waiting to take him fishing, and the two of them spent the rest of the afternoon on the lake. The heat from the sun, the lawn work, and the fresh fish Jennifer cooked on the deck grill that evening left Harrison exhausted and happier than he ever imagined he could be. Then, just as he dropped off to sleep, something nasty crept into his mind.

He tried to make it go away, but it wouldn't. It was a feeling that things were just *too* good. He'd never felt like this before, and what scared him about it was that it seemed someway, somehow, something almost had to happen to restore his life to its natural order.

And that's where his mind dragged him, to a place where all the bad things that ever happened to him were stored up like an attic full of junk, just waiting for him.

A place that was dark and scary.

CHAPTER THIRTY-SEVEN

WHEN HARRISON AWOKE THE next morning, things seemed much better, and as he forked the final piece of French toast into his mouth he began to think that maybe it was just a matter of time, and that he could get used to things being so nice.

Before he left for school, the phone rang and Jennifer held it out for him. "It's my mom."

Harrison blushed and took the phone.

"How are you, Harrison?" Mrs. Godfrey's voice warmed him from the inside out.

Harrison watched Jennifer leave the kitchen. He could hear Coach's footsteps upstairs. He cupped the phone in his hand and spoke softly. "Can things be too good?"

She chuckled. "I'm not sure what you mean."

"Everything is . . . great. It feels like this can't last."

"You'll have to get used to the fact that good things happen to good people. I believe that."

"And I'm good?"

"I wouldn't have sent you to live with my daughter if you weren't."

Harrison smiled. He told her about football and she promised she'd come visit and see a game.

At school, his bright thoughts from breakfast and his call with Mrs. Godfrey were confirmed. There was a lot less whispering and secret pointing than a week ago. Leo Howard still gave him sour looks, but they didn't last as long because Harrison decided to glare right back until Leo looked away. Otherwise he almost fit in. Justin and Becky seemed more at ease around him too, and Harrison began to think that maybe, just maybe, Mrs. Godfrey was right and that he might have found a normal life.

At practice that afternoon, Harrison was finally allowed to hit again, and that's what he did. He felt like a wild animal sprung from a cage. He didn't bother searching out Leo or Leo's buddies. Harrison just clobbered anyone who got in his way. Even Justin tried to tackle him during a scrimmage at the end of practice and Harrison blasted right through him without a second thought.

On their way into the locker room, their uniforms drenched in sweat and their hair matted to their heads,

Justin asked Harrison why he hadn't taken it easy on him.

"Are you kidding?" Harrison asked.

"Not really." Justin scuffed his cleats on the pavement outside the locker room and looked at the ground.

Harrison slapped Justin's shoulder pad. "Come on, Justin, I don't know who's who out there. I got to do my best on every play. I want to be the starting halfback when we play on Saturday. Besides, when I get going, all I see is people coming at me and red."

"Red?" Justin stopped short.

"It's like a mist, a crazy, angry mist."

"That is crazy."

Harrison shrugged and waited for one of their teammates to walk past and into the locker room. "Coach likes it."

Justin rubbed his elbow. "I like it too, but not when you hit me."

"Part of the game." Harrison looked at his friend, hoping he understood. "Right?"

Justin smiled and slapped his back. "Right, and don't worry about starting. There's no way Coach won't start you over Varnett. He's all right, but not even close to you. Hey, I keep meaning to tell you, after the game Saturday there's a big dance. They call it the Fall Ball. Did you hear about it?"

"How would I hear about it?"

Justin tilted his head. "I thought maybe Becky might have said something."

"Why would she?"

"I don't know. Man, she looks like a TV star and she likes you, right?"

"She's nice to me." Harrison's insides tightened.

"So, if she didn't ask you, you gotta ask her," Justin said. "I'm just trying to help. I already asked Charlene Gambol. She's that tall girl with the long, dark hair. We could all hang out."

"I'm thinking about football, not a dance."

"I know," Justin said, "but after we stomp Clayborn Park, you'll want to be at the dance. Everyone will be there celebrating. Come on, that's my job. I'm your wingman."

"Wingman?" Harrison squinted at him.

"Watching out for you so you can focus on the important stuff."

"Stomping Clayborn Park," Harrison said.

"And asking Becky to the Fall Ball." Justin looked past Harrison, smiled, and waved. "Speaking of which, there she is."

Harrison turned around. Becky and two other girls were coming off the soccer field, sweaty with grass-stained knees, giggling together. Becky had a red bandanna tied around her head and it only made her green eyes greener. Fear choked Harrison's throat as the girls approached.

Justin leaned close. "Go ahead, ask her."

CHAPTER THIRTY-EIGHT

HARRISON COULDN'T SPEAK.

"Hey, Justin. Hey, Harrison," Becky said. "This is Delilah and Rachel. Guys, this is Harrison Johnson, the big football player everyone's talking about."

"Nice going on Leo Howard." Delilah was a redhead herself and she spoke without letting up on the gum she chewed.

"Yeah," Rachel said, "I haven't heard him so quiet since kindergarten when he got his tonsils out."

Their words only made Harrison less comfortable. He couldn't speak, but he did manage to nod his head.

"Hey, Becky," Justin said. "Harrison was just going to ask you something. . . ."

All eyes turned to Harrison.

"We were talking about the Fall Ball," Justin said.

Becky suddenly went pale and looked almost as upset as Harrison felt.

"Oh," she said after an uncomfortable silence. "Well, he's probably thinking more about the game than some dance. Well, gotta go. See you guys."

Becky and her friends disappeared before Harrison could blink.

Justin backhanded him in the gut. "You big dummy. What were you waiting for? I set you up perfect."

Harrison swallowed the knot in his throat. "I don't know. I didn't get the chance, really."

"You can't be scared to ask her," Justin said. "She's crazy about you. Did you hear that, 'the big football player'? That's what she called you, bro. She loves you."

"She kind of took off."

Justin waved a hand through the air. "Girls are flighty. Come on, you'll get another chance."

Harrison followed him into the locker room, where they changed into street clothes. Many of the other players had already changed. Harrison felt their eyes on him, but when he did catch someone glancing at him, it was a different look than before. Before, the looks were mocking and mean. Now Harrison could see the uncertainty, even the caution, in their eyes, and he had to admit that it felt good. It made him breathe easier to know that he had a place in this new world where, even if people wouldn't be his friends, at least they would let him be.

"Don't forget we're meeting after dinner," Justin said as they walked out. "I've got two lawns. Meet me at Mrs. Peabody's at twenty-seven Oakwood and I'll get you started. I'll do the other one just down the street. Neither is as big as Doc's, but we only get ten bucks each."

"Ten is great," Harrison said.

"So, I'm not going to Subway. I got homework. See you then, right?"

Harrison bumped fists with his friend and headed for home. He had schoolwork too. Harrison was just finishing up his last math problem at the kitchen table when Coach came in.

"Paperwork for all of us, huh?" Coach said, looking over Harrison's shoulder. "You got number seven wrong. It should be three *x* over fifty-*six*. Seven times eight is fifty-*six,* not fifty-four."

Harrison looked at the last calculation on the sheet and began to erase. "I always mix that up."

"I always used to forget that too," Coach said. "I don't know why. Then someone told me this: five, six, seven, eight, five-six is seven times eight. It's backward, but it works. I don't know. Math is like Chinese to me. That's why I teach English."

"That works. I like it. Thanks Coach."

Coach began taking things out of the refrigerator. "I got a text from Jennifer. She's in a meeting running late, so she asked us to get this started."

Harrison helped prepare dinner by making a salad under Coach's precise instructions. As he cut up a cucumber, he asked, "Do you think I'll start on Saturday, Coach?"

CHAPTER THIRTY-NINE

COACH HAD A HANDFUL of ground beef he was molding into a meatloaf. "Do you think you deserve to start?"

"I'm better than Varnett, right?"

Coach nodded. "Is that all there is to being a starter, just being the best?"

"It should be." Harrison set down the knife and carried the salad bowl to the table.

"What if Varnett started, but you got most of the carries? What would you think of that?"

"I'd like to get all the carries."

"Do you think you'll need the line to block for you?"

"Sure, a little, anyway. I can't run through eleven guys."

"Right." Coach slid his meatloaf into the oven. "Football is a team game. You need everyone working toward the same goal. That's my job, to get everyone working. So don't worry about starting. Leave that to me. Trust me. I want to win, and that's what you want too. You just be ready every time I put that ball in your hands to take it to the end zone. If I can ease you into this *and* keep the team happy, it'll be good for everyone."

Harrison didn't fully understand why all the players—even people like Leo Howard—needed to be happy, or why they wouldn't be happy as long as they won, but he kept his comments to himself, trusting in Coach.

It was dusk by the time he finished cutting the lawn, but he was proud of the job he'd done. The old lady, Mrs. Peabody, tottered out onto her porch after he'd put the mower away in her garage and slipped a ten-dollar bill into his hand. Almost better than the money was the gleam in her eye when she thanked him.

"You're welcome, ma'am," Harrison said.

"You're the new boy, aren't you?"

"Yes, ma'am."

"And so polite. Well, I'm not one for judging people by their past. You just keep doing a good job and people here will like you just fine."

Harrison felt a knot in his stomach and only wanted to get away. "Yes. Thank you."

He backed down the steps, but the woman followed him. "My daughter works at the school. She said you're some kind of violent criminal and not to let you in my yard. I said, 'Pish, he's a *boy*, and I'm not afraid of anyone, not at my age.' So you don't mind folks, you just keep being a nice, polite boy and it'll all pass. It's just a small town."

"Thank you." Harrison hurried down the sidewalk.

The old woman called after him. "It'll pass."

Harrison was out of breath by the time he got home. He let himself into the kitchen through the garage and heard Coach talking on the phone in the other room. Quietly, he closed the door and stopped halfway across the dark kitchen when he heard his name.

"I hear what you're saying, Doc." Coach chuckled. "But they're kids. . . . What? You really want me to *tell* him *not* to ask her? Maybe he isn't going to ask her anyway. . . ."

Harrison staggered back and grabbed the handle of the refrigerator to keep his balance. He felt like a yo-yo, or a Ping-Pong ball, up and down, back and forth, good and bad, bad and good.

"Doc, Doc, all right. Easy. I understand. Yes, I know she's a nice girl and trust me, we all appreciate how nice she's been to Harrison. . . . Okay, Doc. I got it, Doc. Thanks. Yes, good night."

Harrison heard Coach snap his phone shut before he let out a heavy sigh.

"What was that about?" Jennifer's voice came from the front room, where she sometimes liked to do her work at home.

"Oh, Doc and that Fall Ball at school. Seems his daughter is afraid Harrison's going to ask her to that dance on Saturday after the game."

"So?"

Harrison heard Jennifer snap her briefcase shut and then the sound of her entering the living room.

"They're being nice, really." Coach's voice sounded tired.

"Nice? That didn't sound nice to me."

"Well, she doesn't want to have to say no. She's all in tears over it, and you know Doc when it comes to his daughter."

"Then let her say yes."

"I'm afraid that's not going to happen. She already said yes to someone else."

Tears burned the corners of Harrison's eyes as he slipped back out the door and into the dark of night.

CHAPTER FORTY

THE NEXT DAY IN school, Harrison hurried out of his classes so he didn't even have to see Becky. He didn't care that she looked pretty in a turquoise shirt that somehow matched her eyes. The color turquoise made him want to gag. When he walked into lunch and spotted her sitting in the corner where they'd sat together all last week, he went the opposite way and found an empty seat at the end of a table on the far side of the cafeteria.

From where he sat, he could just see her through the crowd. She looked up at everyone who passed by but never scanned the crowd to search him out. His afternoon classes were free from Becky, so he thought he'd dodged her for the day. When the final bell rang, he made his way to the locker room. In the crowded hall he felt a tap on his back. He turned and it was her.

"What gives?"

"With what?"

"I thought you were avoiding me after class, and then you didn't show up in the lunchroom. Is everything okay?"

"Fine." Harrison turned to go.

She took hold of his arm. "Harrison, you're acting like you're mad about something."

"I'm fine." He shrugged her off and kept going.

"Harrison? Tell me. What's wrong? Harrison?"

Harrison spun and clenched his fists so hard his forearms ached. "Don't worry, I'm not asking you to any stupid dance. Dances are for pansies, so you can tell your dad not to worry. And stop sitting with me at lunch. I don't want you and I don't need you."

Becky looked like he'd hit her with a board. Her mouth hung open and her face was all red. Everyone around them stopped and stared.

Harrison growled, then turned and didn't stop until he reached the locker room door, even though she followed him the whole way there. He slammed open his locker and the kids around him got quiet. He yanked his gear out and tugged it on, then laced his cleats and stamped out toward the practice field. When he got there, he kept his back to the school and silently tossed a ball back and forth with Justin until he noticed a couple of the ninth-grade boys looking up the hill toward the parking lot.

"There's your girl for the dance, Varny," Bulkowski said. "And man, she is some girl."

Adam Varnett said, "She's nice, that's what I like."

"I like that blond hair," Leo Howard said.

"You don't get to look, you punk," Varnett said, shoving Leo, who shoved him right back because they were friends.

Harrison turned to see who they were talking about and nearly threw up.

Staring down at the practice field, dressed in her soccer uniform with her arms crossed, was Becky Smart.

CHAPTER FORTY-ONE

THE RED MIST CLOUDED Harrison's eyes throughout practice. On offense, he blasted his teammates with lowered shoulder pads and pumping knees. On defense, he slammed people down to the turf. By the time the team got to its scrimmage period, when Harrison got the ball, his teammates just shied away.

Coach blew the whistle and screamed, "Are you kidding me? Stop him!"

They lined up and Harrison got the ball again on a dive play up the middle. Bulkowski dove at his feet and caught a knee in the head that knocked him away like a fly. The linemen reached out for Harrison's jersey, but he ran right through them. When he hit the secondary, the free safety saw him coming and flinched without even an attempt at a tackle.

Harrison ran all the way to the end zone, turned, and jogged back.

Coach blew his whistle so hard it pierced Harrison's ear. "Everybody, and I mean *everybody*, start running and don't stop running until I say."

The whole team—even Harrison—fell in behind Varnett and started to run laps around the field. Halfway through the first lap, Harrison turned on his speed and passed them all. As he did, Bulkowski said, "Ease up, will you?"

Harrison only ran faster.

Coach let the team keep on running and Harrison lapped them. Finally, seven laps into it, and after three of the big linemen had fallen to the ground, exhausted and panting, Coach called them in and they knelt around him in a tight cluster.

"I have never seen such a disgraceful display as that." Coach glared at them all. "You guys want to beat Clayborn and you're afraid of your own teammate?"

Another time Harrison might have felt embarrassed, but not now. Now all he saw was red.

"He's a freak, Coach." The voice came from the back of the group.

"Who said that?" Coach's eyes darted around. "I said who."

The other players scooted away from Justin to give themselves some distance from the one about to catch the heat.

"Me, Coach." Justin's words could barely be heard. "It's true."

"What does that *mean*?" Coach asked.

"There's no one like him, Coach," Justin said. "Harrison is my friend, but he doesn't care about that or anything. We never had to play a guy like that. He's unstoppable, Coach."

Coach seemed to chew on it. Finally, he nodded his head and his voice came out softer than before. "We still need a better effort. All right, you guys take it in and come back tomorrow with your chinstraps buckled. We've got a lot of work to do."

The team stood and shuffled toward the locker room.

"Harrison," Coach said. "I want to see you."

Harrison returned and stood face-to-face with Coach. Coach put a hand on his shoulder pad. "Don't you worry about any of this. You just keep doing what you're doing. If you were this angry walking around, I'd be worried, but here, on the football field? The players who can bottle that intensity, that meanness, and turn it loose out here? They're the guys who get to one day play in the NFL."

Harrison just stared at him.

Coach tilted his head to one side and let a smile creep onto his face. "You'd like that, right?"

CHAPTER FORTY-TWO

HARRISON DIDN'T SMILE. FOOTBALL was serious business for him, and also for Coach. He spoke in a flat voice and said, "That's what I'm going to do. Football's my ticket, Coach."

Coach nodded and slapped his shoulder pad. "All right, go get changed. I'm going to grade some poster projects in my classroom and I'll meet you home later. Don't worry. The rest of the team will be just fine with you when we beat the pants off of Clayborn."

"I'm not worried."

"Good."

Harrison got changed and left the locker room without speaking or being spoken to. Justin caught up with him when he was halfway across the parking lot. "Hey, wait up. Don't be mad. I didn't mean anything bad, Harrison."

"I know." Harrison kept walking.

"You're not mad?"

"I'm fine."

"Something's up your nose. You've been weird all day. Then you come out here and you're, like, *hurting* people."

"Football's all about hurting people."

"No, Harrison, it's not. Football's about scoring touchdowns."

"People get hurt."

"Right, but that's not the point of the game."

Harrison stopped and clenched his jaw in frustration. "Maybe it is for me."

They walked in silence for a few minutes, burning up the sidewalk, the afternoon sun filtering down through the broad trees that lined the street.

"How come you never talk about your parents, or where you live?" Harrison asked suddenly.

"How come *you* don't?"

They had reached the downtown area, a main street lined with old brick shops and clapboard houses turned into hair salons, insurance offices, and restaurants. Every so often, there were benches people could sit on. Harrison sat down on one and folded his arms across his chest.

"I live with Coach. He and Jennifer, that's his wife, they're my . . . foster parents."

"Coach?" Justin sat down like he'd been hit in the head. "Our coach? You *live* with him?"

"I just told you. He's my foster dad."

"Holy moly, that explains it."

"Explains what?"

"Well, Coach is pretty tough on you. I mean, he's tough on everyone, but the way some of those jerks have been acting toward you? Coach goes crazy when teammates don't treat each other with respect. I mean, really crazy. But you? I guess he doesn't want people to think he favors you when they find out he's your . . . foster dad. Is that like being adopted?"

"No, that's something more. That's like being someone's real kid."

"Sorry. I didn't know. That'd be crazy. I mean, you're pretty old."

Harrison scowled. "It happens sometimes."

"Don't get mad. I didn't even mean you." Justin wagged his head.

"Who did you mean?"

"Well, I live with my grandmother, and she's not too happy about it. She even says so. I never thought there was a way out, that I could get a mom and dad, people to adopt a kid as old as you or me."

"Where's your mom and dad?"

Justin looked down at the sidewalk. "No one knows. My grandmother says my mom's no good anyway. I don't know. Everyone's got some good in them, right? A little? No one ever said anything about my father."

"That's me, too," Harrison said. "Stuff happens."

"Now look at you. After Saturday's game everyone in town will be talking about you."

"Maybe," Harrison said. "I don't know."

"Don't know? Look what you did to everyone today. No one wanted a piece of you, especially me."

"Well," Harrison said, "I guess we'll find out Saturday. I don't know because I've never done it. I've never played in a real game."

"It's all the same."

"Did you ever have the feeling, when everything's going well, like, it can't last?" Harrison asked.

"I think I know what you mean," Justin said.

"Everything seemed so great," Harrison said, "like I was so high up it made me dizzy."

"That's a good thing. That's where you want to be."

"Yeah, but when it's too good to be true, it's because it *is* too good to be true."

"What do you mean?" Justin frowned.

Harrison didn't want to talk about the thing with Becky. Instead, he said, "I just feel like I got too high, and now I'm on my way down. That's why I don't know what's going to happen Saturday. I just hope it's not another disaster. That's what my life has pretty much been—a disaster."

CHAPTER FORTY-THREE

THE BROOKTON HIGH SCHOOL team got clobbered 63–0 on Friday night playing the Clayborn Park varsity team in a sloppy mud game at Clayborn. The rain stopped sometime during the night and the sun broke through the clouds Saturday morning. The day was crisp and clean, perfect for football. Even though it was junior high football, the team got to play on the high school's varsity field. The stands weren't overflowing with five thousand people the way they were on a Friday night for a varsity game, but football in Brookton was big enough that a respectable crowd sat scattered throughout the stands in the sunshine.

Harrison couldn't help himself from searching for Becky's blond hair. He didn't spot her but knew most of the spectators wouldn't arrive until closer to kickoff.

When the Clayborn Park Junior High team got off the bus and marched onto the field like two columns of soldiers—tall, straight, and in lockstep—Harrison's teammates got jittery.

Harrison was standing behind the first-team offense as they ran some practice plays when Justin nudged him. "Holy moly. Check out the size of those guys."

Harrison looked over his shoulder. "Not as big as a thousand-pound dairy cow."

"Dairy cow?"

"I used to work on a farm. Sometimes, for fun, we'd knock the cows over when they were sleeping, till I got beat for it."

Justin gave him a strange look, but Coach called for Harrison to take some turns at halfback with the first team and he bolted into the huddle.

Clayborn won the toss and elected to receive. Brookton's kickoff team let Clayborn return it to the fifty, and it was only three plays later that the Clayborn offense slashed right through Brookton's D.

"Holy moly," Justin said, jogging off after trying to help block the kick on the extra point. "Are you sure those guys are in eighth and ninth grade, Coach?"

Coach gave Justin an annoyed look and sent the kickoff return team out onto the field. Clayborn pinned Brookton down on its own fifteen yard line. Coach sent the starting offense in. Harrison buckled his chinstrap tight, clenched his hands, and bounced up and down on his toes, standing next to Coach on the sideline.

Coach called a toss sweep. Varnett took the pitch and ran for the outside. Clayborn's defense swamped him three yards behind the line of scrimmage.

"Coach," Harrison said, urgent, "put me in."

Coach shot him a quick angry look. "Don't ask me, Harrison. I know you're here."

The words stung.

Coach called a pass play to Justin. The quarterback rolled out and barely got rid of the ball before being smashed to the ground. The pass wobbled through the air and hit the grass near Justin's feet. Harrison started to say something but bit his tongue.

Coach Lee put a hand on Coach's shoulder. "That pass play could work, Coach. Just roll him out the other way. The receiver was open."

Coach clamped his mouth tight, thinking. "No. Harrison, get in there for Varnett. Twenty-three dive."

"Twenty-three *dive*?" Coach Lee's voice rang out. "Ron, it's third and thirteen! You're going to run it right up the middle?"

Coach grabbed Harrison's shoulder pad and shoved him out onto the field. "You heard me, twenty-three dive."

Harrison sprinted so fast to the huddle that he lost his breath. Varnett jogged away after flashing an angry look. Harrison told the quarterback the play.

"Dive?" The quarterback wore a look of disbelief. "You sure?"

Harrison nodded. “Hurry. We’ll get a delay penalty.”

The quarterback called the play and broke the huddle. Harrison got into his position, trying to calm his breathing because he was beginning to feel light-headed, and that only increased his panic and the certainty that somehow, everything was about to fall apart.

He had no time to think. The quarterback barked out the cadence.

“Yellow, seventeen! Yellow, seventeen! Set. Hut!”

Harrison took off for the three hole. The ball hit him in the stomach so hard, what was left of his breath escaped his body in a weak grunt. The crack of pads and the snarls and roars of the linemen filled his ears. Where the three hole was supposed to be was a crouched Clayborn defender, his black-and-orange jersey like a nightmare on Halloween. Before he could take even his first step with the ball, the defender smashed into him full speed.

Harrison closed his eyes.

CHAPTER FORTY-FOUR

THE IMPACT OF THE defender spun Harrison around, but he kept his feet. The only way to go was backward. That's where Harrison went, looping back almost to the goal line, and stretching the defense out over the field.

His instincts took over. Out in open space, he turned on his speed, racing for a small window next to the sideline. The play had broken down completely. Harrison's teammates stopped blocking. All eleven Clayborn defenders were after him. His speed got him back to the line of scrimmage. Two defenders crashed into him, but this time, Harrison had an instant to lower his pads. He got up under them, using his raging bull move, goring them with his shoulder.

The defenders flew through the air.

He turned on the speed again, dodging a third

defender and gaining ground upfield. Another defender dove at his legs. Harrison's powerful knees, churning like a factory machine, smashed the player's helmet and he dropped to the grass. Harrison had the first down now, but he kept going.

When he stopped to juke another defender, two more jumped on his back, clinging to him like cobwebs. He surged forward and took them for a ride. The added weight slowed him enough so that two more defenders caught up and tangled his legs enough to bring him down. The whistle blew and the referee ran up to spot the ball.

Harrison climbed off the grass and tossed the ref the ball.

The ref looked at the field judge and said, "Did you see that?"

The field judge could only shake his head.

Harrison jogged back to the huddle. His offensive teammates slapped his shoulder.

"Nice run," the quarterback said.

Coach signaled in the play. The quarterback called a twenty-eight sweep, then scolded his line. "This time, you guys get some blocks for him, will you?"

The offensive linemen grunted and nodded their heads.

The team went to the line and the quarterback barked out the cadence, took the snap, then pitched the ball to Harrison. Harrison took off, this time in more open space to begin with, this time with his teammates making some blocks. He ran through one defender, over another, and past two more.

Touchdown.

Harrison took care to hand the ball to the ref, who said, "Nice run, son."

The offense stayed on the field and Harrison ran it in for the two-point conversion, giving Brookton an 8–7 lead. Harrison jogged off, heading for Coach.

Coach didn't even seem to notice him. He was busy giving the kickoff team instructions. Harrison hung near him, quietly accepting the praise of his teammates and wondering if he'd done something to displease Coach.

When the kickoff team jogged off and the Brookton defense took the field, Harrison stood right next to Coach so that he couldn't miss him. Coach kept his eyes on the field, though, consulting with Coach Lee, who signaled in the defensive plays. Even though Clayborn marched down the field, the Brookton defense held on the ten, and Clayborn was forced to try a field goal, which sailed wide to the right.

Harrison and his teammates cheered from the sideline as the kick wobbled crazily off to the side of the goal posts. Harrison tugged his helmet on, buckling it up to get ready to run out onto the field with the offense.

Coach yelled, "Give me the starting offense."

Harrison paused and gave Coach a questioning look.

"Not you, Harrison," Coach said. "I want the starters.

Varnett, get in there."

Harrison bit down hard on his mouthpiece to keep from shouting something he shouldn't. Varnett jogged past him and slipped into the huddle with the rest of the Brookton offense. Harrison clenched his hands and watched. The first play was an inside trap. Varnett gained a yard. The second play was a toss outside.

When Varnett picked up a first down, the crowd and the team cheered, but Harrison felt sick. It wasn't fair. After the two runs he'd just made, it wasn't fair that Varnett got to benefit from the team's momentum. The next play was a pass to Justin, which he caught on a crossing pattern over the middle. The twelve-yard completion gave Brookton the ball on the thirty-four yard line with another first down.

But, just as suddenly, the Clayborn defense exploded, dropping Varnett twice behind the line of scrimmage and leaving Brookton with a third down and fourteen yards to go. Coach called a time-out and the offense jogged over to the sideline to hear what he had to say. Harrison stayed close.

"Okay," Coach said. "I'm thinking Varnett on a toss. Leo, can you seal that outside linebacker to the weak side?"

Leo Howard played tight end—half receiver, half lineman, and the widest lineman in the offense's formation—and he nodded his head violently. "I got him, Coach."

"Good," Coach said.

The quarterback raised his hand. "Uh, Coach. No offense, but why wouldn't we give it to Harrison?"

Everyone turned to look at him as Harrison's heart pumped excitement through his veins.

CHAPTER FORTY-FIVE

"YOU WANT TO GIVE it to Harrison?" Coach's voice was stern, and he gave no sign of what he preferred to do. It was a real question.

The quarterback looked around. Varnett and Leo were the only ones who sneered at him. The line and even Bulkowski nodded with wide-eyed enthusiasm.

"*Yes.*"

"*Yeah.*"

"*Please.*"

Coach paused, then said, "Okay, Harrison, get in there. Twenty-seven sweep. Get us a first down."

"How about a touchdown?" The words leaked out of Harrison's mouth without him even thinking.

Coach seemed to be fighting a smile. "I'll take a touchdown, sure."

The offense jogged back out to huddle up behind the line of scrimmage. The quarterback repeated Coach's play. They broke the huddle and went to the line. At the snap, Harrison took off. He snagged the pitch out of the air, tucked it tight, and flew for the edge of the formation.

The outside linebacker that Leo was supposed to block came through clean. Harrison saw Leo lying almost comfortably on the ground and he couldn't help thinking that Leo had simply let his man through to give him a clean shot at Harrison's knees. Harrison darted his head and shoulders inside, then let his legs launch him outside. The linebacker whiffed completely, wrapping his arms around a puff of air.

Harrison kept going. A cornerback took a shot at his legs. Harrison's knees pumped like race-car pistons. He felt a bang and saw the cornerback drop like a swatted fly. A lineman on the loose had an angle on Harrison. The sideline was so close he'd have to go through the player if he was going to score. Harrison lowered his shoulder and blasted through the defender.

The grunt of air leaving the lineman's body sent a shiver of pleasure through Harrison's frame. There were more defenders coming, but he didn't have to mess with them. Instead, he put on a burst of speed and had enough time to look back before he crossed into the end zone. The crowd went wild.

Harrison returned the ball to the ref, who said,

"Another one, son. You can carry the rock."

In the huddle, the quarterback called a twenty-three dive for the two-point conversion. Harrison plowed through the defense like a lawn mower through a leaf pile and put Brookton up 16–7. This time, when Harrison jogged off with his teammates slapping his helmet and shoulder pads and the crowd standing on its feet stomping the metal bleachers in a thunderstorm of noise, Coach met him at the sideline.

Instead of slapping his back, Coach grabbed either side of Harrison's helmet and pulled his face close. Instead of a jubilant grin, Coach's face was tight, his eyes wide and lit with craziness, even tears.

His voice was a roar. "Harrison!"

CHAPTER FORTY-SIX

HARRISON HAD GROWN USED to hearing his name shouted, growled, and spit out like a curse word. That was the path life had led him down. So he couldn't say Coach's expression and the sound of his voice were unfamiliar, even if they were completely unexpected.

"What, Coach? What did I do?"

"What did you do?" Coach's eyebrows disappeared up under the bill of his cap. His voice burst forth like floodwaters. "What didn't you do? You did everything. You ran. You hit. You dodged and spun and stiff-armed. You were perfect, Harrison!"

Coach's face trembled, but not with rage. His eyes stayed wide, hovering just outside the metal cage that protected Harrison's face. "You're *unstoppable*."

"Why aren't you smiling, Coach?"

Coach blinked and drew back as if he'd been sprayed. "Smiling? I can't smile. I'm amazed. I'm floored. I'm shocked."

"You seemed mad." Harrison didn't take his eyes off of him.

"Mad? No, no." Coach shook his head. A smile erupted on his face, a big, toothy, tongue-wagging smile. He held his face close and whispered. "Don't you see? If it had been *me* putting you in there at that critical time, they never would have accepted you. But *I* didn't ask for you to go in; *they* did. Your teammates. They practically *begged* me."

Coach laughed, and Harrison did too.

"Come on," Coach said. "Let's go break Clayborn's chops."

Chops were broken. Harrison ran for three hundred and thirteen yards. The final score was 56–21 and, in the end, it was the Brookton team—instead of Clayborn—who tackled Harrison to the ground with everyone laughing and reaching out just to touch him.

Harrison laughed until he cried.

It wasn't until he was home with Coach and Jennifer that the joy of the victory melted away enough to allow other thoughts to creep into his head. The three of them sat together on the living room couch watching a movie. Jennifer must have read his expression.

She reached across Coach and tapped his arm.

"Whatcha thinking about, Harrison?"

"Nothing." He didn't want to spoil the evening. "Just football."

"Oh," she said. "Good."

Harrison returned his attention to the movie. Jennifer reached for the popcorn bowl and offered him some before she put her head back down on Coach's shoulder.

He decided that he really didn't even feel that bad about missing the dance. He couldn't dance anyway. It wasn't until he lay awake in bed that the image of Becky slow dancing with Adam Varnett flooded his mind. He turned over and pulled the sheets tight, comforting himself with the thought that Varnett couldn't be having too much fun after losing his starting job.

The next day Harrison, Jennifer, and Coach put on nice clothes and walked to the big stone church that stood guarding one end of Main Street. Church pushed Harrison into a daze. All the singing and prayers, the soft words and the fiery ones, were things he just didn't get. What made this time different was the minister talking about *him*. The sermon was about new beginnings and how everyone can find the right place if they'll just try to work hard and believe. The minister didn't say Harrison's name, but it was him, Harrison was sure.

He said, " . . . or a boy who comes from another place and finds his gift is to play football, and he runs for three hundred and thirteen yards and all of a sudden, his life is *different*. He may not be different, but his life is, because everyone around him sees him as something new, a new beginning."

Jennifer shook Harrison's knee and winked at him, then tried not to smile.

On the walk home, Coach said, "The last player to make Reverend Lindsey's sermon went on to play four years at Notre Dame."

"Did he make it to the pros?" Harrison asked.

"Not the pros, no. He's a heart surgeon."

"I'll make the pros," Harrison said.

"You never know," Coach said.

After lunch on the deck out back, Harrison changed his clothes and cut lawns with Justin, who couldn't stop talking about the game. Harrison was just happy he didn't talk about the dance. The third job on Justin's list was Doc Smart's.

"I thought he didn't like you to do it on Sundays," Harrison said.

Justin shrugged. "Not when he's around. He likes the peace and quiet, but he said they've got two weddings to go to today, and the grass grew fast this week. We're good, just like last time, as long as we're done before he gets back home."

"Well, I'm glad they won't be there," Harrison said.

"She looked miserable, you know," Justin said.

"I don't even know who you're talking about."

"All everyone talked about was you and us beating

Clayborn. I think Varnett was drinking or something. He got sick in a trash can by the door. They left early."

"Drinking?"

Justin shrugged. "I don't know. It's crazy. Maybe he wasn't. That's what people said."

Harrison could only shake his head. That only made it worse, worse that Becky would go to a dance with someone that stupid, someone that out of control. If he'd been caught, Varnett would have been kicked off the team. Becky certainly wasn't what she first appeared to be, that was for sure. Either way, Harrison wasn't happy to see Doc's Suburban roll into the circular drive before they'd finished the job. He kept his head down, focusing on the last bit of trimming as Doc's family piled out of the SUV and went inside. He was just putting the weed-eater away when he heard them leaving again. After the sound of the engine disappeared down the driveway, he snuck a peek at the big white house with its unblinking black shutters, empty windows, and proud brick chimneys.

Until yesterday, he never thought he could belong in a place like that. His place was outside with the dirt, grass, and weeds. Now, though, with the sound of the crowd still ringing in his ears, it didn't seem impossible that one day he would live in a house like Becky's, the house of a doctor, a lawyer, or a pro football player.

Back home, Coach invited him to go fishing. They did, and as the sun sank low in the sky, Coach steered the boat toward the end of the lake where a pier jutted out from a busy public park. The noise of barbecues and happy people floated toward the cloud-ribbed sky.

Coach hopped out onto the dock and pointed to a cluster of huge old trees where a large white tent dressed in pink and white bunting sat like a birthday cake. The sound of violins drifted from the tent. "Look, a wedding or something."

Harrison helped tie up the boat.

Coach offered to buy ice-cream cones at a concession stand not far from the pier, and Harrison's stomach rumbled at the thought. As they waited in a short line, Coach gave Harrison a ten-dollar bill and excused himself to use the bathroom.

Harrison stood alone, studying the flavors on the board. He ordered a triple chocolate with sprinkles for himself and a single butter pecan for Coach. He stuffed some napkins in his shorts pockets, then paid for the cones. After taking one in each hand from the woman behind the counter, he walked out into the slanted sunshine and scanned the crowd in the direction Coach had disappeared. When he felt a tap on his shoulder, he spun around too fast, bumping into someone and knocking the triple ice cream off his cone. It landed with a splat.

Flustered, Harrison looked up, only to be shocked by who he saw.

CHAPTER FORTY-SEVEN

BECKY WAS WEARING A pink dress with flat white shoes that looked like ballet slippers. Her hair was pulled up in a band of tiny white flowers. A smear of chocolate ran down the front of the dress, leading to the rapidly melting ice cream on the hot concrete.

"I'm sorry about your ice cream," she said.

"Sorry about your dress." Harrison wiped his forehead on his arm, carefully balancing Coach's butter pecan, and looked away. "What are you doing, anyway? I thought you were afraid of me."

"Why do you say that?" she asked.

"Why?" Harrison spit the word out.

"That's right." She crossed her bare arms and tilted her head. "Why?"

Harrison turned to face her, dazzled by how pretty

she looked. The sun tinted her face red, a wisp of blond hair escaped the flowers and framed one side of her face, and her eyes were like frozen emeralds.

"You were so afraid I'd ask you to the dance. That's right. I heard your father talking to Coach."

"No." She shook her head. "You don't understand."

"I understand plenty." Harrison scooped up the fallen ice cream with a napkin and dumped it in a trash barrel.

"I asked my father to stay out of it," she said.

"After you told him I scared you."

"I *didn't*. He heard me talking to Rachel. I was crying, but not because I was afraid of you. It was because I *didn't* want to say no to you."

"You've got a boyfriend. Go tell him."

"I *don't*."

"So you're a liar on top of it all? You're going to tell me that Adam Varnett isn't your boyfriend?"

"No, he's not. He's my friend. Our families are friends. He asked me before you even came here. My father said I had to go, because I made a commitment. Trust me, I wanted to go with *you*."

Harrison's heart skipped a beat. He wiped his fingers on another napkin and kept the sour look on his face.

He handed her a napkin. "Here. Can I help?"

Harrison dabbed at the worst of the chocolate mess. Becky took his hand and hugged him before stepping back.

Coach appeared and cleared his throat. "Becky."

"Hi, Coach. We had an accident. I was just telling Harrison that it's okay."

Harrison couldn't speak, and his face felt hotter than the sun as he handed Coach his cone.

Coach licked melting butter pecan around the edges as his eyes followed the chocolate trail down the front of Becky's dress. "Your father's not going to be happy when he sees that mess. Are you in the wedding?"

"They already had the ceremony and the pictures, so it's okay." Becky's smile made the ice-cream stain seem smaller. "Congratulations on the win, Coach."

"Thanks. Come on, Harrison, let's get you another. Bye, Becky."

Harrison stared at Becky. She tilted her head and gave a small wave. He waved back and turned to go, catching up with Coach as he got into the back of the line. Harrison snuck a look at Becky as her blond hair and pink dress wove through the crowd before disappearing into the big tent.

"You don't have to get me another one, Coach," Harrison said, his mind automatically adding up the money it was costing the Kellys to support him, despite the big win.

"They'll give us one if we tell them it fell off the cone. Don't worry."

The two of them didn't speak until they were back on the boat. Harrison worked hard to keep the rapidly melting ice cream from dripping on his hand. He used his free hand to untie a mooring line while Coach got the other one. They climbed aboard, Coach fired up the engine, and they chugged away from the pier. Out in the middle of the lake, Coach cut the motor. Even from there Harrison could still see the tent and catch wisps of its music.

Coach took a bite of his cone and asked, "Can we talk?"

CHAPTER FORTY-EIGHT

THE SUN SAT LIKE an orange Buddha on a bed of heavy clouds. Its light gave Coach's face a golden glow. Waves lapped the boat's aluminum skin.

"Sure," Harrison said.

"About girls?"

Harrison looked at his feet in the boat's bottom and scuffed at a stray piece of fishing line.

Coach hesitated before speaking. "It's better to wait for that stuff, Harrison. It complicates things. That's all."

Harrison couldn't look up. "I like her."

"I like her too. She's a pretty girl. Be friends. Don't get involved. Trust me. I've been teaching eighth grade for a long time, and before that I was an eighth grader myself. Trust me."

"I do trust you . . ."

"But?" Coach asked.

"I . . . she . . ." Harrison shook his head. "I really like her, Coach."

"Like her, like how?"

"It's like a bomb went off in my chest."

Coach let out a long sigh. "I'm not sure her father would appreciate that. I just don't want to see you get hurt."

Harrison looked up. "You can get hurt playing football."

"Not like this you can't. It's worse . . . but it happens. I just wanted to warn you, Harrison. I'm not trying to tell you what to do. I just care."

Coach tucked the last bit of his cone into his mouth and started the motor.

Neither of them talked to Jennifer about what had happened with Becky. She teased Coach about his fishing techniques while they ate, and by the time she served them chocolate cake and cold glasses of milk, Harrison wasn't even thinking about Becky and the pink dress.

They watched *Sunday Night Football* until the third quarter. When Green Bay went up by thirty-five, Coach stood and said, "Big week this week, so let's get you rested up. Me too."

Jennifer rolled her eyes. "Every week's a big week to Coach."

"Weldon has the best quarterback we'll see all year." Coach wore a serious face. "And a defensive end that we'll be lucky to block with two guys."

"Oh, football." Jennifer waved her hand, put down her book, and got up off the couch. "Football on TV. Football in your brain."

"Yeah, football, right, Harrison?" Coach winked at him. "We are on a roll. I can see the playoffs. I can see the championship."

"I love it, Coach," Harrison said.

Jennifer twisted her lips. "How about reading a couple chapters before you go to sleep?"

"I will," Harrison said.

Coach said, "Well—"

"Uh!" Jennifer held up one hand to stop him. "School first. Books first. Next time, shut the game off at half-time."

Coach knew better than to argue. Harrison felt warm inside just being around two people who were kind and affectionate and sometimes funny.

At breakfast the next morning, while Coach was in the shower, Jennifer moved the frying pan off the burner and turned off the stove. Instead of serving the eggs she'd scrambled, she sat down next to Harrison at the table and covered his hands with hers. She caught Harrison's eyes, and for a moment he felt like he was looking at Mrs. Godfrey instead of her red-haired daughter, because their eyes were the same.

"Harrison, you like it here with us, don't you?"

Harrison's stomach turned over because he couldn't help thinking that this was it, the bad news that would put his life back into the awful balance he was so used to. He nodded his head.

"Well . . ." She looked past him, out the window, and tears filled her eyes. "I hate to upset you, but I need to ask you a favor."

CHAPTER FORTY-NINE

HARRISON BRACED HIMSELF. "OKAY."

She took a deep breath and held it for a beat before setting it free. "Harrison, I know you have a mom, and no one can ever replace her."

He frowned and shook his head. "She's gone."

"But she's your mom, and I don't ever want you to think I don't know you loved her, and you'll always love her."

"What do you want?"

She squeezed his hands. "I think you can see how much I care about you. You don't have to do this, but I want you to start thinking about calling me 'Mom.' It would mean a lot to me, and that's what I want to be."

Harrison dropped his eyes. He let her hold his hands, even though his finger joints began to ache. He couldn't look at her when he said, "What if something happens? What if I can't stay here anymore?"

A short, puzzled laugh burst from her throat. "What? Why would you say that?"

He shrugged. "I never stay anywhere."

"You can stay here as long as you want, Harrison. I promise."

He looked into those green eyes. "Your mom said she never broke a promise. She said she's been lucky that she never had to."

A tear spilled down the side of Jennifer's nose. She sniffed and nodded. "I've been lucky too, and now I'm lucky because I've got you."

"Mom," Harrison said, testing the word. He smiled, and this time he used it to mean her. "Okay, Mom."

His new mom hugged him tight.

CHAPTER FIFTY

FIVE WEEKS WENT BY and in that time, Harrison not only got used to calling Jennifer "Mom," he couldn't think of calling her anything else. He also stopped worrying that he'd wake up and it would all be gone. On the football field, he kept getting better and the team kept winning. Mrs. Godfey came, as promised, and watched him play in their last regular-season game. Afterward they had dinner at home, just the four of them.

"Oh my," Mrs. Godfrey said, "you really are quite the football player. I heard people talking in the stands. What were they calling him?"

Harrison's mom wiped her mouth on a napkin. "Unstoppable, Mom."

"Yes." Mrs. Godfrey's eyes sparkled and she nodded with approval. "Unstoppable."

The word "unstoppable" got printed next to his name in the local paper, and more than once. Most of his teammates began to admire him openly. Those who didn't—like Varnett and Leo Howard—were too nervous about his viciousness on the practice field to say anything at all.

Harrison worked hard off the field as well, with Justin. Even though cutting lawns had ground to a halt because of the changing weather, Justin had lined up an endless supply of odd jobs they performed in the evenings and—when they had time—on the weekends. Harrison had a wallet fat with over two hundred dollars in it, more than he ever could have imagined.

In school, he sat with Becky every day at lunch. They texted each other when they weren't together, and sometimes they even held hands under the table at Subway. Her father seemed okay with the two of them being good friends. He even complimented Harrison's growing statistics of touchdowns and rushing yards.

When Becky had a birthday dinner at a Japanese steak house with her mom and dad and ten other friends, including Justin, Harrison got to sit right next to her. When she opened the present he bought with his lawn money, she sniffed and wiped the corner of one eye as she fastened the necklace around her neck. Harrison blushed and had a hard time getting to sleep that night.

Harrison wasn't the only one soaking up the football

glory. People began talking openly to Coach about how obvious it was that he'd get the varsity job next year. Brookton Junior High won its first two playoff games. If they could win the semifinal game against Larsonville, they'd be in the championship and play at a nearby college stadium where thousands were expected.

To get ready for the semifinal game, Coach decided to have a live scrimmage at the end of Thursday's practice. Harrison ran all over his teammates, but Coach was careful to call some pass plays and other plays that let Harrison's teammates in on the action as well. Late in the scrimmage, the quarterback completed a pass down to the two-yard line.

Coach blew his whistle. "Okay! Defense, you hold them on this play and you don't have to run sprints. Offense, you score and you watch the defense run ten cross fields."

The defense groaned because they all knew they'd likely have to stop Harrison.

"Let's go!" Leo Howard screamed. His face turned purple. He slapped the shoulder pads of his teammates to urge them on.

Coach called a simple off-tackle run play, giving the ball to Harrison. The other players in the huddle chuckled with glee. Harrison lined up and bolted forward at the snap of the ball. He took the handoff and lowered his shoulder. A defensive tackle shot through the hole Harrison was supposed to run through. He blasted the defender and sent him flying, but more defenders were on his legs.

Harrison churned forward. A cornerback darted in from the outside and jumped on his back. Harrison kept going.

With three defenders on him, he plowed into the end zone. Just as Coach blew the whistle to signal the touchdown, Leo Howard launched himself low—helmet first—and smashed into the side of Harrison's knee. Harrison went down. Coach's whistle shrieked again, signaling for the second time an end to the hitting.

The defenders climbed off him, and Harrison sprang to his feet and bounced on his toes, delivering the ball to Coach.

"You okay?" Coach asked Harrison, then scowled over at Leo.

"Fine." Harrison wasn't going to admit that he felt a sharp twinge in his knee.

CHAPTER FIFTY-ONE

HARRISON KEPT THE WORRY off his face. Hiding his true emotions reminded him for the first time in many weeks of his life with the Constables, people with whom he hid his true feelings on a daily basis. It made him uncomfortable to revert back to his old habits, but Harrison had heard Coach scolding the other players often enough to know that football was a game that required one to get over the discomfort of little bumps and bruises.

He kept as quiet as he could at dinner, but when Coach or his mom asked a question, he was careful to reply with a flowery enthusiasm that disguised his concern. He knew how much Coach was counting on a win, so he waited until his mom was taking a bath and Coach was in his office, lit by the ghostly light of his video screen, before sneaking into the kitchen to fill a plastic grocery bag with ice from the freezer. With the covers over his legs, Harrison sat in bed, reading and icing his knee.

The cold made the joint ache even more, until after about fifteen minutes, when everything went numb. He got lost in his book, and when his mom came in to kiss him good night, he made a tent of the blanket with his other knee so she wouldn't notice the lump from the ice bag. When everything was quiet, he slipped into the bathroom and dumped the melted ice into the toilet before flushing it down and stuffing the wet bag into the bottom of the garbage.

From time to time in the middle of the night, the dull pulse of pain in his knee would wake him up, but he could always drop right back off. Friday's practice was a walk-through, with no real running, so Harrison was able to disguise his discomfort. He iced the knee again Friday night and felt better by Saturday morning.

Then, on the bus ride to Clayton Park—the neutral site where the game was to be played—the knee began to throb once more. When he saw the banners flapping in the breeze, though, and the bright-colored cheerleaders' pom-poms in the sunshine, Harrison nearly forgot about the pain.

The pregame talk Coach delivered to the team helped him as well.

"This is a tough game," Coach growled at them right

before kickoff as they crowded around him. "It's for tough people, tough men. That's right—men. It's time. You're not boys anymore. You're young *men*, and that's how I need you to play. . . . If you do, we'll be playing in the championship next Saturday, so dig down deep and play like a *man*."

The entire team went wild, and the emotion carried them through the kickoff and into the first defensive series, where they crushed the Larsonville offense. After a punt, Harrison took the field with the rest of the Brookton offense. The first play was a toss sweep to Harrison, and he forgot all about his knee. He dashed for the sideline at the snap. The quarterback pitched the ball to him. He snatched it from the air and turned on the speed. The defenders came at him like a video game, but Harrison dodged and weaved like a man among boys. One final defender dove at his legs before he crossed the goal line, but Harrison leaped through the air and landed in the end zone for the touchdown.

The jolt in his knee cut through the excitement. Harrison gritted his teeth and tried not to limp. His teammates swarmed him, cheering. He jogged with them to the sideline.

Coach grabbed his arm. "Great run. Are you hurt?"

"I'm fine," Harrison said. "Tweaked my knee a little, but I'll walk it off."

"You sure?"

"Sure. Fine."

Harrison dug deep and played like a man.

As the game wore on, the ache in his knee got worse. Harrison was able to mostly ignore it and comfort himself with the fact that they were winning and he could ice it all next week before he had to play again. There was no way he couldn't gut it out for seven more days if it meant winning a championship and getting Coach the job he always dreamed of. Coach deserved that.

Harrison ran for five touchdowns and Brookton won 42–20. The dull throb in his knee cut through the celebration on the bus ride home, not because of the pain, but because it made him worry that something might really be wrong. Harrison thought of the look he wore in the Constables' milking parlor to keep from getting whipped and—as he'd done so many times in the past—kept a false smile plastered across his face. It scared him that for the second time in a few days his thoughts had wandered back to his past life. Sickness and dread flooded his body and mind. He closed his eyes and prayed it didn't mean something bad.

CHAPTER FIFTY-TWO

AT HOME, HARRISON PRETENDED to be exhausted and used that as an excuse to go to bed early. He packed his knee between two bags of ice he'd managed to smuggle out of the kitchen. The pain was like a little toothache in his knee, not enough to keep him from sleeping, but he didn't sleep well. The next morning his bed sheets were soaked from the leaky bags. He gobbled down three Advils in his bathroom and tried to force himself to walk downstairs without a limp.

"You okay?" Coach sat at the breakfast table and looked up from the morning paper.

"Sure." Harrison slipped into his seat. "A little sore from the game."

"What a win, right?"

"Awesome."

When his mom appeared, he could tell by the look on

her face that something was wrong. "Um, Harrison? I don't want to embarrass you. Things happen to everyone sometimes. Did you have a problem last night?"

He shook his head. "No."

"Well, your sheets are . . . um, wet."

His face felt hot. "I didn't . . ."

"It's okay. If it happens to you sometimes, I just want to know so I can put something underneath the sheet. I don't care, I just don't want the mattress to get ruined."

"I didn't wet the bed, Mom."

Coach and his mom stared at him.

"Well, how come your bed is all wet?" she asked.

He shook his head. "I'm fine. It was just some ice."

"Ice for what?" Coach set the paper down.

"My knee is a little sore, that's all. It's nothing."

"Why didn't you say that?" his mom asked.

"Coach said to play like men. I played with it. I just wanted to ice it a little."

"Let me see." His mom put her hands on her hips.

"I'm fine."

"So, I can see."

Coach stood up and came around the table. "Harrison."

Harrison sighed and slid back his chair. Coach knelt down and rolled up the leg of his sweatpants. Harrison winced.

His mother gasped. "Oh my God."

CHAPTER FIFTY-THREE

THE KNEE WAS RED and swollen like a grapefruit.

Coach poked gently at the puffy red skin.

"Play like *men*?" His mom didn't hide her disgust.

"It's okay, Mom." Harrison poked it too. "It barely hurts."

Coach ignored her. He asked Harrison to get up and move around. Harrison stood and bobbed up and down, dancing across the kitchen floor, refusing to wince.

"See?"

"That doesn't hurt?" Coach asked, with hope in his voice.

"Just a little. It's a little ache is all. I can run with it, though. We've only got one game left, Coach. Then I've got all off-season to rest it."

Coach opened his phone and dialed. "Doc? Yeah, it's

Ron Kelly. I hate to bother you again on a Sunday, but can you take a look at Harrison's knee for me?"

Harrison worried about his knee on the drive over to Doc's, wondering if this would be the thing that returned his life to its original gloom. He comforted himself with one good thing, though, and texted Becky to let her know he'd get to see her. They went into Doc's office and Harrison sat on the edge of the exam table. Doc came in, dressed in church clothes. Becky followed him and stood in the doorway. Harrison grinned at her until she blushed.

"Okay, you," Doc said to his daughter as he gently closed the door, "you said hello. Now go help your mom and let me take a look."

Doc asked Harrison to walk back and forth across the exam room floor.

"Okay, not too bad," Doc said before pointing to the table. Harrison hopped back up and the paper crinkled beneath him. He tried to ignore the sterile smell of alcohol. Doc poked at the knee. He took the leg in his hands and gently bent and turned the joint. When he twisted it one certain way, Harrison winced and grabbed it.

"Sorry," Doc said, gently returning Harrison's leg to the exam table. "Well, I think you may have a small tear in the cartilage."

Harrison felt a jolt of panic, until he saw the relief on Coach's face.

"He can play with that, right, Doc?" Coach said.

"Oh, sure. He moves fine. We may want to rest it and ice it this week, take it easy. Saturday's the championship, your last game, right?"

"It is," Coach said.

"It's not going to feel good, but if he rests it and ices it, I think there's a good chance he can play," Doc said. "Then we can take some time and determine whether it needs surgery or not. What I do want to do, though, is send him in for an MRI. I'm pretty sure it's just the cartilage, but it's always better to take a look, in case I'm missing something."

"Sure, Doc," Coach said. "No problem."

A knock at the door revealed Becky, her face still blushing, or blushing again. "Mom said I could show Harrison my new Koi fish when you're done."

Doc twisted up his lips. "Okay, but show him quick. We've got church and they're going to the hospital."

Harrison was proud at the expression of shock Becky wore at the word *hospital* because it proved how much she cared about him.

Coach and Doc shared a glance between themselves. Coach smiled and said, "He's fine, just a precaution."

"Can you play in the championship?" Becky asked.

Harrison hopped down. "For sure. Come on, show me that fish."

Becky led him around back to the decorative pond that was part of the pool area. A fountain trickled into a large, shallow stone basin filled with fat lily pads and what appeared to be oversized goldfish. Becky shook a handful of pellets into her hand before tucking the jug away in the outdoor cupboard at the base of a small cabana. She tossed the pellets into the pond and the water thrashed with fish fighting for the food. Among them Harrison saw the new one, white, pale and sleek, bigger than the rest, a length of living muscle. Its fins waved through the water like bed sheets on a windy line. It cut a wide path among the other fish.

"He's kind of like you on the football field." Becky stared at the Koi. "The new guy, making everyone else look bad."

"It's not just about making people look bad." Harrison remembered Justin's words. "It's about scoring touchdowns and winning games. There's skill, too."

"You know what I mean." She slipped her hand into his, intertwining their fingers. "You're the best, that's all."

Doc called Becky's name and their hands flashed apart. Harrison followed her around to the front, got into the pickup with Coach, and waved good-bye, his eyes holding on to hers until the bend in the driveway.

"How was the fish?" Coach smirked at him.

"Big."

"Uh-huh." Coach nodded his head and turned on the radio. "Doc got us right in."

The hospital was forty minutes away. Coach called Jennifer to tell her what was happening. Harrison rode with the window down and flexed his hand in the current of air. For the end of October, it was a warm day.

The MRI took nearly a half hour, and Harrison had

to lie still in a banging tube. He felt like a hot dog in a bun, but they played music for him and let him choose the station. It seemed like every other song reminded him of Becky, and Harrison wondered if he was too young to be in love.

They were back in the truck and on their way home when Coach got a call. He kept driving and answered it. After identifying himself and giving a couple of one-word answers, Coach slowed the truck down and pulled over to the side of the road.

His hand clenched the phone, and his face lost its color. "Are you sure? Could it be a mistake?"

Harrison felt a brick in his stomach. He wasn't sure why.

"Yes," Coach said, "we'll be right there."

When Coach looked over at him, the tears in his eyes scared Harrison more than anything in his life, ever. The image of Mr. Constable and the belt flashed across his brain.

"What? What's wrong, Coach?"

Coach reached out and pulled Harrison to him. "Oh, my son. My beautiful son. I love you so much."

Coach was crying, and it scared Harrison so that his throat knotted up and tears began to stream down his own cheeks.

"Coach, what's wrong? Can't I play?"

Coach hugged him even tighter. "I don't know, Son. Maybe, but maybe not. It doesn't even matter."

CHAPTER FIFTY-FOUR

THE NEXT TWO DAYS were a blur.

The injury wasn't the problem. He had a slight tear in the cartilage that could be fixed anytime. Everyone called the injury a blessing because it led to the discovery of something that might have gone unnoticed until it was too late.

There was something on his knee, on the bone. That's what they called it, "something." They didn't call it a tumor, and no one said the word *cancer*. Still, somehow Harrison knew in his mind that's what it was. Cancer.

He knew by the look on his mom's face, the red around her eyes, and the way she held her chin at a ferocious angle that seemed to challenge the whole world. She didn't cry in front of him, even though it wasn't hard to tell she had been crying before. It made Harrison feel better that she didn't cry. It made him feel like things might be okay.

They told him from the start that they were going to operate on him as soon as possible, and that made sense to Harrison.

The only question he could ask the doctor was, "Can I still play football?"

The doctor, tall with pale skin and sunken cheeks, patted him on the shoulder and tried to smile. "Let's hope so. No promises, but let's hope so."

The day of the operation, Harrison lay in his hospital bed and reminded his parents of the doctor's words. "He said he hopes so, Coach. I should be okay. I'll be back."

Coach took his hand and knelt down beside the bed. "Harrison, can you call me Dad? Not all the time, but sometimes. Can you do that? See, I think of you as my *son*. I know I should have said it a long time ago, because that's the way I felt, and when you get out of here, we're going to make it legal. We're going to adopt you, Harrison. Is that all right with you?"

Harrison's throat felt tight. "If I can't play . . . you don't have to keep me."

Coach glanced at his wife before his glistening eyes locked onto Harrison. "No, no, you don't understand. Of course we'll keep you. We'll keep you no matter what. You belong to us, Harrison, and we belong to you. Please, Son, don't say that. I hate that I let you think it."

Harrison's embarrassment was drowned out by pure joy. "I'll be okay. I promise, Coach . . . Dad."

The nurse came in. She put a needle in Harrison's arm and the fog of the past few days evaporated. He knew exactly where he was. His entire life fast-forwarded in his brain and it made him want to cry. The needle stung, but after the plastic bag swinging above his bed dripped cool liquid into his veins for a few minutes, he began to feel light-headed and peaceful. He let his head settle down into the deep, clean-smelling pillow.

They wheeled him down a long hall and into another room. They put a mask on his face, and the room began to spin around, and Harrison thought of the big white fish, so much bigger and stronger than the rest.

Unstoppable.

Just like him.

Then everything went dark.

CHAPTER FIFTY-FIVE

HIS DREAMS WERE BAD.

Finally, he opened his eyes and saw his mom and Coach—his dad. They looked tired, but they smiled at him and touched his face, and Harrison felt hopeful.

His leg itched.

Harrison tried to sit up. His mom raised the bed for him and she put a straw to his lips so he could sip cranberry juice.

"Itches." Harrison reached for his leg. Panic filled his mom's eyes. Harrison felt for the itch below his knee. His fingers groped at the blanket.

Something was wrong. Something was very wrong. A nurse came in and fiddled with the plastic bag over his head. He felt like he was losing his breath and he lay back and began to relax. He slept to the sound of his parents' voices. They were talking to a doctor.

When he woke the next time, he was hungry. They fed him and talked to him and they seemed nervous for a reason he couldn't name. For two days he was in and out of sleep, but he mostly slept. On the third day he felt alert when he woke. His parents slept in two big chairs at the end of his bed. They held hands in their sleep across the gap. Coach needed a shave.

Harrison smiled at the thought of teasing him.

His leg itched and his knee ached in a way he hadn't imagined it could.

When he reached for his leg, he bumped the thick bandage around his knee and winced. Tears of pain pooled in his eyes. He reached over the bandage and tried to scratch his itching leg. He knew it was there, under the sheets somewhere, and the past two days of not being able to find it and scratch that itch all came back to him.

The moments stacked up like the cars of a train wreck, piling into each other, one after another in quick succession, wreaking more havoc with each new crash.

Panic stole his breath.

Harrison heard a scream and he knew it was his own.

The sound ripped his parents from their sleep.

"My leg!" The voice was ragged and torn; he barely recognized it.

"Momma!" He had never called Jennifer that before;

Mom, yes, but not Momma, and she rushed to his bed to hold him tight.

He pressed his face into her chest to muffle his scream. "My leg is gone!"

CHAPTER FIFTY-SIX

DURING THE NEXT FEW days at the hospital, Harrison didn't really want to talk. He would watch TV, movies mostly. He nearly forgot about the game, until Coach came in on Saturday with the whistle around his neck. The fact that the team lost didn't matter. It also didn't matter to him who was there with him, even though his mom and dad usually were. Justin didn't matter. Doc. Even for Becky he could only muster a weak hand squeeze before the TV drew him back into its blinking world.

The day after the game, he was watching the Turner Classic Movies channel when he saw an old black-and-white picture about a submarine. When the Japanese hit the sub with depth charges—bombs shaped like barrels dropped into the sea—water began to surge into the ship, filling it, crushing everyone inside until only lifeless hands and faces with wavy blurs of hair floated across the screen. Harrison snapped off the TV as the credits rolled.

"That's me." He said it to himself, but his mom looked up from her book.

"Honey?"

Harrison shook his head. He didn't have the energy to explain that the ocean of fear and misery that was his life had only been held back by the walls of something man-made, like the metal skin of a submarine. The protection that held everything back was football, a made-up game that people loved to play, watch, and talk about.

It held back all the evil in Harrison's life, and Harrison had come to think that life on his new submarine was the natural state of things. It wasn't. The natural state was for him to drown in a briny soup, to be crushed by it and forced to breathe it in until he was as useless as a floating body.

"Honey?" His mom wore a worried look.

Harrison sank his head back into the pillow and rolled his head to the side, away from her.

His leg was gone from the knee down and his hospital stays had just begun. They told him that over the next few months he would spend a couple of days in the hospital every other week for chemotherapy. Harrison had bone cancer, and it might have spread through his body already, into other bones that might have to be removed. As bad as it was to be a cripple, Harrison knew it was ten times worse to have cancer. Cancer was evil. Cancer ate away at you from the inside out, until you were dead. Over the next several days they brought doctors and counselors and shrinks and even Reverend Lindsey to his bedside. They tried to coax, shame, and urge him to look at the bright side. There was no bright side, only pain and misery.

Then Major Bauer arrived.

CHAPTER FIFTY-SEVEN

COACH NEARLY JUMPED OUT of his chair. The major had to brace up when Coach threw himself into the old soldier's arms. They patted each other's backs the way a cowboy might thump his horse's neck.

His mom stood. "Kirk!"

The major hugged them both.

Major Bauer looked older than in his picture. His hair had begun to turn gray, his beard was gone, and his tan face wrinkled at the corners of his dark eyes and mouth. He stood straight and tall, though, and when he finished greeting Harrison's parents with kisses and hugs, he marched up to the side of Harrison's bed and held out his hand.

Even in his miserable state, Harrison couldn't refuse the iron grip. Despite his serious face, Major Bauer's deep, dark eyes brimmed with kindness.

"I heard I'm needed." The major looked around the room, and his eyes came to rest on the stump that was once Harrison's leg. "And I see that I am."

Harrison shifted in his bed and reached down to itch the missing leg. Suddenly it felt like his leg—from the knee to his foot—was being crushed, stabbed, and burned at the same time. Harrison cried out and reached for the missing limb. The pain ripped a hole in his pride and he wailed for it to go away.

As the wave passed, Harrison was surprised to realize it was Major Bauer holding him and not his mom. His grip was as gentle as it was strong.

"It'll pass." The major spoke soft as a nurse. "It'll pass."

Finally, Harrison's heart slowed.

"There," the major said, releasing him. "Phantom pains. The nerves will fire like your leg's still there. Nothing quite like it. Trust me, I know."

Harrison tilted his head at the old soldier. Major Bauer smiled, stood, and tugged at his left pant leg. A chrome joint gleamed just above the shoe. Jutting straight up from that was a shiny, thick metal rod. Harrison thought of a magician he'd seen on TV, an illusionist, but the leg really was metal.

"The latest and greatest." Major Bauer pulled his pant leg all the way up to the knee, showing off a chrome piston and yet another shiny joint. "Yours will look a lot different. You're lucky. There's a lot more you can do when you've got an upper leg."

The major winked at him and dropped the pant leg.

Harrison's spirits were lifted by the sight of the soldier. He was strong and handsome and he moved through the world as if nothing was missing. Then Harrison thought about what his life had been for a brief couple of months—his life as an athlete, a football player.

His face fell, and he looked away.

"Hey," his mom said. "The major is talking to you."

"Won't be the first young man to look away from me." The major's voice was soothing as he spoke to Harrison's mom. "Harrison? Harrison, will you look at me?"

Harrison couldn't resist.

"You can come back from this," the major said. "I know you're pitying yourself right now. Next you'll get depressed, then angry, but it'll all pass. It will. I've seen it many times, and I've lived it myself."

"I can't come back and play." Harrison glared up at Major Bauer.

"Play?"

"I'm a football player. They said I was unstoppable." Harrison ground his teeth together.

"Football?" Major Bauer put a hand to his chin. "I don't know, but let me show you something, okay?"

Harrison just stared.

Major Bauer had a shoulder bag Harrison hadn't even noticed. The old soldier set it down on the windowsill, then removed an iPad and switched it on. He fiddled with the screen for a few moments, then held it out for Harrison to see.

CHAPTER FIFTY-EIGHT

HARRISON STUDIED THE PICTURE of a man in a ski cap, red jacket, white winter gloves, and dark blue sweatpants running down a desert highway. Beyond him lay low hills spotted with scrub brush beneath a pale and empty sky. Protruding from the cut-off end of his right pant leg was a chrome football-shaped thigh with a mechanical knee and a yellow shock absorber for a shin. The man's young face looked strong and determined.

"Who is that?" Harrison asked.

"Jeff Keith. The first above-the-knee amputee to run across America."

"Run?"

"San Francisco to Providence. Thirty-four hundred miles."

"How?" Harrison stared at the picture.

"He just did it. Here, look at this." Major Bauer's fingers scrolled through his iPad before he showed Harrison another picture.

"Is that him?" Harrison studied the old newspaper photo of a young man playing goalie in a lacrosse game. Across his chest it said BOSTON COLLEGE. His legs were covered in baggy cotton sweatpants, but Harrison could tell the right one was stiff and unnatural.

"That was with a *wooden* leg, a division-one college athlete. Lost his leg, like you, only a year younger, when he was twelve. Also bone cancer, like you. Look at this quote. I love this quote.

"'Believe in the incredible and you can achieve the impossible.'"

Harrison huffed impatiently. "It's not football."

Major Bauer took the iPad back. "Yeah . . . look at this."

This time he handed Harrison the picture of a football player in an electric blue uniform with one leg in the air, marching in a high-step toward the camera.

"There's nothing wrong with him," Harrison said.

"Except his lower right leg is missing."

Harrison looked closer.

"His name is Neil Parry. He played for San Jose State." Major Bauer sat down on the side of the bed and put a hand on Harrison's shoulder. "I'm not making any promises, Harrison, but I want you to know you're not alone, and some of the people who are like you have done some amazing things. The technology gets better every year. Maybe you can do what they did, or maybe you can do more."

Harrison looked back at the football player. Major Bauer reached over and scrolled through the other pictures too. It was like an escape hatch. Suddenly, in the dark crushing flood inside his submarine, a light appeared. It was like Major Bauer was thrusting a life jacket at him, something that would propel him up, out of the darkness and the dead floating bodies to the surface above, to light and air.

Harrison grabbed hold.

CHAPTER FIFTY-NINE

MAJOR BAUER TOOK A four-month leave from the army. He moved into the small apartment above the Kellys' garage and was with Harrison in the hospital for the better part of every day. The nurses, doctors, and therapists treated him with high regard, and that was because they all soon learned that he ran an amputee rehabilitation program for the U.S. Army. The major would sometimes try to let the therapists work on Harrison's leg, but inevitably he ended up taking over in a way that no one seemed to mind.

Having someone as important and strong and smart as the major working on his leg made Harrison proud, and it went a long way toward making him feel better. Several days after the major arrived, it was time for Harrison to be done with the painkillers. His leg still ached, but Advil seemed to be enough, and he liked having the fog clear from his brain. That Saturday, he was scheduled to go home.

When Coach walked into the hospital room that morning, he wore a brand-new Brookton Junior High Football sweatshirt.

"What's that for?" Harrison asked.

"It's the mock-up for our football gear next year. We're getting a whole new look. The uniforms will have the same styling. You like it?"

Harrison scowled. "You went all the way to the championship and they didn't give you the varsity job? Did anyone tell them you lost your running back?"

"Sure. Everyone knew. So even though we got embarrassed 63–7, they offered me the varsity job."

Harrison's mouth hung open. "But that says Brookton *Junior* High."

Coach laughed and pushed a wheelchair over to the side of the bed. "Now's not the time for me to take the varsity job. I told them maybe in two years."

"Coach, you said that was your dream."

Coach's face turned serious. "I'm not just your coach. I'm your dad. If you're going to make a comeback, that's the team I want to coach, not varsity."

Harrison looked out the window. The bare trees reached for the sky with silver fingers. He nodded his head. "Good."

They helped him into the chair, then the car, and

finally into the house. Coach parked in the driveway and helped him up onto a pair of crutches while Jennifer fretted at them to be careful of his leg. Harrison set his jaw and crutched his way up the blacktop. Major Bauer greeted him at the mouth of the garage, arms folded across his chest, and dressed in a T-shirt and shorts that showed off his chrome leg before it disappeared into his track sneaker. Harrison moved inside and his eyes adjusted to the cavelike gloom. Spread out around the concrete floor were parallel bars, ramps, rubber tubing, barbells, weight machines, and a massage table.

"Welcome home," Major Bauer said. "Now let's get to work."

CHAPTER SIXTY

THE MAJOR SHOWED HARRISON'S parents into the house before he lifted two dumbbells off the rack and lay down on a bench. He pressed them up and down, exhaling as he counted out the reps, ten in all. Metal clanged as he replaced them and pointed toward the bench.

"You get on and I'll hand you the weights."

Harrison lay down and took a set of smaller dumbbells from the major. He tried to do what the major had done, but his arms wobbled and the weights swayed all over the place.

"You'll get it," the major said. "It takes time to train your muscles. Just work through it."

The major counted the reps out loud. At seven, Harrison began to struggle and strain.

"Come on!" the major shouted. "Don't quit!"

The word *quit* sent a shiver through Harrison and he groaned with effort, refusing to give up. The major helped him with his last few reps, urging him on with barks of praise.

"Good! Good! That's the way to work!

"Now this," the major said, pointing to a flat bench with a padded roller at one end connected to a stack of weights by a cable that ran beneath the bench, "is your bread and butter machine, the leg curl. This will make your hamstrings strong—the back of your leg—and you'll need that now more than ever. First we walk, then we run, then . . . if we're lucky, you learn to cut."

"Cut?"

"If you're serious about football, you can't just run in a straight line. You've got to be able to plant your foot and redirect at a new angle—that's a cut."

"I get it. And I can do that?"

"If you're strong enough, I think I can teach you." The major planted a thumb in his own chest.

Harrison nodded, got on, and curled the roller toward his butt by squeezing his leg. He ground out twelve reps.

"Good," Coach said. "Next time, we'll bump up the weight."

They moved from one exercise to another, and just when Harrison thought there wasn't anything else they could possibly do with the weights or the machines, they ran through the whole thing again.

They worked until dinnertime. Sweat drenched Harrison's clothes. Major Bauer finished with a therapy session on Harrison's leg, massaging it, then tapping the skin and gently rubbing the end of his leg with a cloth before washing it and binding it tight.

"What we need," the major said as he worked, "is for this skin to get desensitized. This skin has to be tough and durable—not now, but when you're fully healed. This skin has to be . . . oh, heck. Here, look at this."

The major whipped off his own prosthetic as if it were nothing more than a sock, and he held up his stump for Harrison to see.

CHAPTER SIXTY-ONE

HARRISON WINCED, THEN LOOKED apologetically into the major's eyes.

"It's okay, you'll get used to it. It's your life now, Harrison, just like it's mine. We can run, but we can't hide. I tell all my men that."

Harrison looked back at the stump and the smooth, leathery skin.

"You ought to just touch it. This is from decades of work, but we'll get you there. It's got to be your interface with the prosthetic, so it has to be smooth and strong and durable. It won't happen overnight, but this is where we're headed."

Harrison reached out and touched the smooth, cool surface. It felt more like wood than skin.

"You know why humans rule the earth?" The major

tugged his prosthetic back into place.

"Because we're smart?" Harrison said.

"Because we're *adaptable.*" The major danced a jig on the garage floor, his sneakers scuffing in perfect rhythm. "We can adapt to almost anything. That's why we survive. That's why we *thrive.* You're going to adapt to this. Just watch."

The door leading into the kitchen opened. Jennifer stuck her head into the garage and told them to get washed up because dinner was almost ready. The major went up the stairs to his apartment and Harrison went inside to use the kitchen sink.

After dinner, Harrison was exhausted. They had moved his furniture and all his things down to the first floor in the room with its own bathroom that had been Coach's office. He climbed into his own bed, thankful for the fresh cotton smell of the sheets and the hiss of the wind through the big pine trees outside the window.

"Mom? Can I get a TV in here? Just while I'm getting better?"

His mom looked around the small room. "Maybe. Actually, I was thinking about all that TV in the hospital. I know you were bored, but it didn't seem to help."

"It kept my mind off all this." Harrison covered a yawn.

His mom reached down beneath the bedside table and brought out one of the Louis L'Amour books, *The Warrior's Path.* "Just give this a try. I know you liked the first two. If you can get into another one, I think it'll be ten times better than the TV. Just try."

She pointed to the shelf below the tabletop. "Look, I got you the whole set, so when you finish this—"

Harrison took the book. "I just think it's going to be hard to concentrate."

It wasn't hard. After the first two pages, Harrison lost himself in the story. When he woke in the middle of the night, the book lay on his chest and the reading lamp warded off the darkness creeping from the corners of his room. He needed Advil. His mom had left him two with a cup of water on the table. He gulped them down and took a big drink, then lay back again.

In the morning, while his parents went to church, Harrison and Major Bauer began their work. The major attached rubber tubing to Harrison's injured leg and had him strain against the tubing from every angle.

"This leg has to be able to work ten times better and harder than it used to, so we want every muscle, ligament, and tendon, every fiber of it, to be stronger." They worked his good leg as well, for balance. The session ended again with a rigorous massage.

They had roast beef and mashed potatoes at midday and then worked again in the afternoon. A lot of the exercise in the afternoon focused on Harrison's upper body and his core because the major said he needed his whole body to be strong. They did every kind of situp Harrison could imagine and then some more. They worked his lower back, lifting weights off the floor, and wedged into what the major called a "Roman chair," where Harrison's body hung off the edge of a padded rail and he could raise and lower his torso like a door hinge. Again sweat soaked Harrison's clothes, and the major ended it all with the massage.

"I thought a massage was supposed to feel good." Harrison winced as the major worked his fingers into the healing skin.

"You know what feels good about rehab?" The major looked up and raised his eyebrows.

"What?"

"When you're done. That's about it. And now . . ." The major wiped his hands on a towel. "We're done."

Coach went out back in his jacket and cooked burgers on the grill for dinner. After a blessing, Jennifer said she hoped the major wasn't overdoing it. He and Coach waved her off.

"This is what he does, honey. Relax." Coach slipped a hamburger off the big plate he'd brought in from the grill and onto a bun before loading it down with a bit of everything.

"There's time," she said.

Major Bauer raised his head from the table like a dog who'd detected an intruder. "Not much time. Not if he's going to play next fall. We've got a tight schedule."

She frowned and dished some coleslaw onto her plate, tapping the last shreds of cabbage loose with the spoon so that the clacking sound got their attention.

"I don't know if it's about football right now. Oh,

Harrison," his mom said, "please don't look at me like that. I just don't want you to get your hopes up."

"Hope?" The major made a puzzled face. "Hope is the fuel of recovery. We got to keep his hopes up, Jennifer. Hunger and hope, that's what drives a man."

"Kirk, I can't tell you how much it means to all of us that you're here and willing to help," Jennifer said, "but he's *not* a soldier. He's a thirteen-year-old boy."

Harrison didn't know what to say, and by the quiet sound of ketchup being squirted onto buns and silverware clinking against their plates, no one else knew what to say either. After dinner, Harrison hobbled to his bedroom on the crutches and flopped down on his bed. He didn't want to think about the friction between his mom and Major Bauer, so he picked up his book. He only had four chapters left.

Two pages into the book, there was a knock at the door. It opened a crack and his mom peeked in. "Harrison? Someone's here to see you."

As the door swung slowly open, Harrison launched himself off the bed. He flew across the room with one hop and fell against the door, slamming it shut as he fell to the floor.

"No!" His voice was so loud it shocked even him. His leg thumped with pain. "Get out of here! Leave me alone!"

CHAPTER SIXTY-TWO

"HARRISON? IT'S ME." JUSTIN'S voice sounded sad and weak through the door.

"It's okay, Justin." Jennifer's voice was soothing. "I'm sorry. I didn't know he wasn't ready to see anyone."

"It's just me, though. I tried to text him. His phone is off."

"I think he knows. Come on."

Harrison listened to their footsteps and then the sound of the front door before his mom said good-bye. Harrison clambered to his feet, locked the door, and hopped over to the bed. He took up his crutches and hurried to the front window, where he pulled aside the curtain. Justin had his hands in his pockets. His chin sagged to his chest. As he shuffled down the sidewalk, he kicked a stick and looked back through the evening light at the house.

Harrison dropped the curtain.

A soft knock sounded at the door.

Harrison returned to the bed and lay down.

"Harrison?"

He said nothing.

"I'm sorry. I didn't know you didn't want to see anyone." His mom's voice barely made it through the door.

"I don't want anyone to see me." Harrison stared at the ceiling. "Not now, not ever. I'm a freak."

After a time, his mom said, "I love you, Harrison. Call me if you need me."

The floor creaked beneath her feet as she walked away. Harrison reached over and turned out the light. He lay quietly, thinking. He'd forgotten about his phone. It lay on the bedside table. He thought about Justin's words and wondered if Becky had tried to text him too.

He rolled away from the phone. He didn't care. He didn't want to see her, either. He was a cripple now, and soon he'd be bald and a perfect freak show. Harrison squeezed his eyes shut tight and the tears spilled out of them onto his pillow. His leg began to throb—not the stump, but his leg, his missing leg. His whole body began to tremble and the sobs clawed their way out of his chest, wave after wave, until he finally fell asleep.

CHAPTER SIXTY-THREE

THE KNOCKING ON HIS door sounded like small explosions. Harrison bolted up, his leg aching.

"Harrison! Let's go." Major Bauer's voice held no pity and he rapped again, shaking the doorknob. "We've got work to do."

Harrison slid out of bed and used the crutches to help him across the room to unlock the door. Major Bauer barged in.

"You sore today? That's good. Means you're working."

Harrison flopped back down on the bed. "Did you know I start that chemotherapy stuff on Friday?"

"What's that got to do with this?" Major Bauer wore Army fatigues and an olive-green T-shirt. His arms were dark with hair and he folded them across his chest, scowling.

"What's the use? I'm going to be puking all over myself, bald as a bat, and skinny as a string bean. Why should I do all this bull?"

Major Bauer nodded his head as if he were hearing something for the first time. "That's right. You'll get sick and lose your hair, and you'll get weak. But strength is like money in the bank. You put more in, and when you got to take some out, you still got some left. You put a little in, you take the same amount out, and you're bankrupt. We're going to put money in the bank. You really don't have a choice, pal."

Harrison scowled right back at him. "I used to live in a place where they told me what to do like I was a dog. Coach and my mom aren't like that. You can't just *make* me."

The major sat down on the end of the bed and put a hand on Harrison's good leg. "You know why I'm here?"

Harrison shrugged.

Major Bauer pointed up at the ceiling. "That man saved my life. There were almost two hundred Republican Guards surrounding us. We lost five men. Four of us were wounded. Coach and two others loaded the three other wounded guys into a gunship. They thought I was dead. I looked like it. The chopper was taking on fire and the pilot wanted to get out of there. Coach held a gun to his head and wouldn't let him leave until all the bodies were on board. I was one of those bodies, alive, barely. My leg was scorpion food, scattered all over the sand. Do you know how long that man wished for a son? And then you came, and he didn't believe it could happen, not with a thirteen-year-old boy . . . but it did."

Harrison swallowed, and shook his head. "I'm not really his son."

The major stared at him, hard. "You don't really believe that, do you, pal?"

Harrison looked down. "No."

The major gave his leg a squeeze. "Come on. I heard you were unstoppable. Let's see it."

Harrison got up on his crutches and followed Major Bauer into the kitchen. The light coming through the windows was gray and weak. The major had boiled eggs, toast, and orange juice all laid out. They ate in silence, then headed for the garage and got to work.

Becky showed up that night after dinner.

CHAPTER SIXTY-FOUR

HARRISON WAS IN HIS room. Dinnertime had come and gone. Coach brought home a new Mac laptop after school, and Harrison spent the afternoon exploring the internet. He was busy on the computer when his mom knocked softly and came in.

"No surprises this time," she said. "But Becky is at the kitchen door."

"She saw all my stuff?" Harrison was thinking of his rehab equipment.

His mom shrugged. "Can she see you? I think it would make you feel better."

Harrison's heart was thumping. He pulled the covers aside, then tucked his legs in, rumpling the spot where his missing leg should be; finally, he put a pillow down over it so that if someone didn't know, they might think he hadn't lost his lower leg at all.

Harrison took a deep breath. "Okay."

His mom bit her lip and disappeared.

Harrison tapped on his computer until he heard the soft shuffle of Becky's feet and the uncertain steps she took across the living room floor. Then she appeared in the doorway like an angel, bright and soft and lovely to look at. In her hand was a small bouquet of flowers.

"Hi." She smiled at him like nothing was wrong, extending the flowers. "You were out of it in the hospital."

"Sorry about that." He spoke without any real emotion as he took the flowers and set them on the lamp table. "Thanks for visiting me."

"Of course I visited. Um . . . Justin was pretty upset in school today."

"Who do you think this is harder on? Justin?" He pointed to his missing leg beneath the sheets.

"Well, thanks for letting me in."

"Yeah, well, I've got to show you something. I go for chemo on Friday. I guess I'm pretty sick."

She looked down at her shoes. "You don't look sick."

"I will. Soon. I doubt you'll want to see me then."

"Why do you say that?" She looked up at him, confused.

"Look." Harrison turned the computer screen for her to see.

Becky took a step backward and gasped.

CHAPTER SIXTY-FIVE

"YOU SEE?" HARRISON HELD his chin high. "I told you."

"Who is that?" Becky pointed at the screen.

"That's me. That's what I'll look like. Scary, right?"

She shook her head.

"Yes, it is," he said.

"What is that, Harrison?"

"It's called Face Morph. You take a picture of yourself and you can do things with it. I made me bald, which I'll be. Skinny, which I'll be. Pale, that too. Tired. Exhausted. Ugly from pain, and probably suicidal."

"You're scaring me."

"I'm scared."

"Why are you doing this?"

"Because I'm not Harrison, the new kid in town who scores seven touchdowns a game. That's over. . . . I'm a freak. And you need to know it before you come in here with your stupid flowers acting like nothing's wrong. Just get out."

Becky took a step back and searched his face. "Really?"

"Really." He tried to melt her with his glare.

Her shoulders slumped. She turned slowly and reached for the door.

He opened his mouth to speak.

Nothing came out.

She stepped through the door, but he knew if she looked at him, she'd come back. That's what he wanted, more than anything. He just couldn't ask. So with all his might he willed her to look back at him.

The door began to swing closed.

CHAPTER SIXTY-SIX

THE LATCH CLICKED INTO place like a firing squad.

Harrison winced.

Her footsteps crossed the living room. The front door screeched open and banged shut. The whisper of her shoes on the concrete walk faded into the night.

CHAPTER SIXTY-SEVEN

MAJOR BAUER RODE WITH Harrison and his parents to the hospital on Friday and accompanied them all the way to Harrison's room. There was another bed there besides his. A suitcase rested against the wall. A Sony PSP along with a teddy bear anchoring a bunch of "Get Well" balloons sat on the night table. The sheets were rumpled and Harrison looked around for his roommate.

The nurse saw him looking. "Oh, that's Marty. He's in therapy until lunch. Let's get you into a gown."

The nurse said she'd be back and disappeared. Harrison sat on the edge of the bed and let his mom help him out of his clothes and into the hospital gown. His fingers trembled as he tied the cloth ties together.

"Here," his mom said, "I can do that."

Harrison snatched it away from her. "I got it. Thanks."

Major Bauer clapped his hands and looked around. "Well, I'll go see if I can scare up your therapist and get her mind right. I don't want them babying you just because of a little chemo."

Harrison's parents watched the major go, and neither of them looked like they knew what to say when he'd gone. His mom sat down on the bed and held Harrison's hand. "It's going to be all right, Harrison. You're going to be fine."

"They said I'm gonna be pretty sick."

Coach put a hand on Harrison's head. "Good thing you're tough."

Harrison shook his head. "Am I going to wear a wig?"

"Do you want to?" his mom asked.

Harrison ran a hand through his short hair. "I like my hair this way."

"Then I'll get you one just like it," she said.

Harrison looked at Coach. "The championship was pretty ugly, huh?"

"What made you think of that?" Coach asked.

"Just me, losing my leg. All this. We would have stomped them."

"I know we would have."

"Next year," Harrison said.

Coach looked like he might cry, but he nodded hard instead. "That's right."

The nurse came back and stuck an IV needle into Harrison's arm. The clear liquid dripped from the bag on its hook above and Harrison could feel the cool salt water flowing into his arm.

"Well," Coach said, extending a hand for Harrison to shake, "I'm off to school. Go get 'em, Son."

Harrison kept his chin up, but when his father walked through the door, he felt only half as strong. His mother squeezed him tight, as if she had read his thoughts. A doctor Harrison didn't recognize came in and introduced himself as Dr. Kirshner. His hair was gray and thin, and he wore glasses that made him look as smart as he sounded. His voice was gentle, but he spoke in clipped sentences, where every word meant something. He explained—more to Jennifer than to him—that the medicine they were about to give him would kill all the newly forming cells in Harrison's body.

"We think the tumor was contained." Dr. Kirshner wriggled his nose to work the glasses up higher on his face. "But with this kind of cancer, we know chemotherapy increases a patient's chances by a significant factor."

Harrison swallowed at the word *chances*. They all knew what it meant.

The nurse injected another clear liquid into his IV line, something they said would make him relax. He went into a kind of daze that lasted until he realized a technician was injecting a tube of sparkling amber fluid into his IV line.

"It's going to feel a bit cool," the technician said. "Maybe a tingling."

Harrison realized she wore a wig herself and that her eyebrows were nothing more than skid marks of colored pencil on her brow. Something in her eyes said she was sorry as the cool tingling crept up Harrison's arm and into his heart. He lay back and half closed his eyes, tears turning everything into a kaleidoscope of colors.

His mom held his hand tight.

CHAPTER SIXTY-EIGHT

HARRISON PRETENDED TO SLEEP, but he was really listening.

His mom talked in a low voice to the nurse about the boy named Marty.

The nurse said, "Please, Mrs. Kelly. We do this all the time. It's hard at first, but we know it helps for children to see other children who've been through the same thing, and Marty is so upbeat. Trust us."

Harrison kept his eyes shut, wondering what it was they did all the time and whether or not he could avoid it. He didn't feel that bad so far, just a heavy weight in his stomach, nothing he couldn't get along with. He heard the door swing open and the rattle of wheels. He snuck a peek at the gurney a male nurse wheeled in like a librarian making a delivery of books.

It wasn't books he delivered.

Between the two nurses, they carefully lifted Marty off the gurney and into the bed. The rails clacked into place and Harrison heard the hum of the bed's motor as someone raised it up.

"Hi, I'm Jennifer Kelly. Are you Marty?"

The sound that answered Harrison's mom shocked him. The words hummed across the room with an electronic buzz. They were in the voice of a space-age robot.

"Yes. I am. Marty. Very nice. To . . . meet you."

Harrison's heart began to pound a bit harder. He couldn't keep his eyes closed and he stretched his neck to see.

"Oh, Harrison, you're up. Harrison, this is Marty. Marty, my son, Harrison."

Marty's face was big and round, and he was bald. His ears stuck out and his enormous eyes blinked at Harrison. Marty's skin was as pale as a sea creature's and his body was a skeleton. He held what looked like an electric shaver to his neck, just along the lip of a long red scar that ran from the bottom of his chin down to his chest.

"Nice. To meet you . . . Harr-i-son." The shaver buzzed. *"They said. You are. A foot. Ball. Player."*

"I . . . was."

"What school?"

"Brookton." Harrison realized his voice was barely a whisper.

"Well." Marty's machine buzzed and his bird's chest heaved up and down with the exertion it took for him to gulp out the words. *"I go. To Mason. Maybe we. Will play. Against . . . each other. When we. Get out. Of this place."*

Marty's big round face was as bland as his electronic voice, but his eyes glittered like diamonds in the sunshine. Harrison couldn't tell if Marty was joking or not.

Marty put the shaver back to his neck. *"You look. Very strong. They said. You scored . . . forty-six. Touchdowns. I would. Hate to. Have to. Tackle. You."*

Harrison couldn't help liking him. He smiled at his mom, then at Marty.

"They are. Trying. To make. Me." Marty raised a scrawny arm. *"Into. A . . . body builder. I am. Going. To take. A nap. Nice. To meet. You."*

"Nice to meet you, too."

Marty nodded once, then lay his big head back into the pillow. He swapped his voice machine for the bed control. The motor hummed as it laid him flat. He closed his eyes and appeared to be asleep before the bed hit bottom. The nurse pulled the curtain around Marty's bed.

Harrison tried to watch TV.

Fifteen minutes into an old black-and-white show called *The Rifleman*, Harrison started to throw up. Marty stayed quiet behind his curtain through it all. Harrison wondered if he was asleep or just hiding from Harrison's loud groans and the terrible retching sounds. When Major Bauer appeared in the afternoon, Jennifer whispered to him and he went away looking disappointed.

Harrison wanted to die.

Dr. Kirshner appeared and looked at the nurse's laptop. He talked to Harrison's mom, then examined Harrison before he said, "I've got something I think will help. Hang in there."

In just a few minutes, the technician with the wig returned with a small vial of clear liquid. She injected it into Harrison's IV line, offered him a smile, and went away. Ten minutes later, Harrison began to feel better.

Soon Coach arrived along with Major Bauer. When they learned that Harrison was feeling better, they smiled at each other.

"Good," Coach said, "because we've got some great news."

CHAPTER SIXTY-NINE

THE MAJOR STEPPED UP beside Harrison's bed, iPad in hand. "Look. It's the J72. I got it. *We* got it."

Harrison looked at the picture of a stainless-steel leg. It looked similar to what he'd seen the major pull off his own leg.

"Like yours?" Harrison asked.

"Better." Major Bauer beamed. "It's the Army's latest and greatest. This is one of the very first. I had to pull some strings. You can't believe what this baby can do."

"Play football?"

"Maybe dance in a ballet." The major did a pirouette with his hands up over his head.

Coach laughed, but Jennifer frowned and spoke in a hushed voice. "All this talk about football. I wish you two would stop."

Coach looked from her to the major. "Fuel for recovery, right?"

"Well," the major said, taking back his iPad, "I'll let Harrison get some rest. Feel better, buddy. You and I will be breaking a sweat before you know it."

"Why, Mom?" Harrison asked, puzzled by the frown that remained on her face.

She sat down on the side of his bed and ran a finger through his hair. "Everyone wants you to get better, Harrison. That's what's most important. Football is a long way away. We just want you to be well, and there are no guarantees. I don't want you to get your hopes up too high."

"But I can do it." Harrison looked at the men and thought he saw the major give a small nod. "I *will* do it."

"If anyone can, I know it will be you." Doubt stained her words.

"Neil Parry did it at San Jose State. Major, didn't you show her?"

His mom gave the major a quick scowl before her face returned to him and softened. "That boy lost just part of his lower leg, Harrison. Your operation was different."

"But the . . . that J72. No one had that before."

"I'm just saying that it's very difficult, and it hasn't been done. And, no matter how good the J72 is, it won't be the same. I'm sorry, but the doctors have told us that the truth is best."

“But I could *play*.” Harrison’s voice came out quiet but hard at the same time. “Coach said I could. The major said.”

“That’s what we’re all hoping for,” his mom said.

“That’s what we’re working for,” the major said.

“You can do it,” said Coach. “I know you can.”

His mom glared at his dad, but this time Coach didn’t back down.

CHAPTER SEVENTY

AFTER TWO DAYS, HARRISON was ready to go home. He said good-bye to Marty and couldn't help asking his roommate when he was leaving.

Marty's eyes widened and he shook his head slowly, pressing the voice machine into the scar alongside his throat.

"I hope. Not too. Soon . . . Harr-i-son. I like. The food. Here."

Harrison looked at Marty, reading his eyes for the joke, before he grinned and hobbled away on his crutches.

The major kept Harrison busy at home with the weights and bands and machines, grinding out reps like Olympic athletes in training. Everything Harrison did, the major wrote down. Harrison realized the major had been doing so since they started, and when he asked why, the major gave him a funny look.

"You got to have a plan." He showed Harrison the grid of exercises and the numbers that filled each little individual box. "Otherwise, how do you know where you're going? Here, look. I probably should have shown you sooner, but these workout cards are just automatic for me."

Harrison studied the names of all the exercises he'd been doing and noted the increase in the amount of weight he was using on certain machines. "I'm getting stronger."

"Yes, you are." The major put the card into a folder and tucked it away on a shelf above Coach's tool set. "You should be proud."

Harrison smiled.

The massages still hurt, even though the skin on the end of his leg was toughening up nicely. It wasn't all physical work for Harrison. The major also helped him with the schoolwork that Coach started bringing home for him so he could keep up to speed with his studies. All that work left Harrison weary and ready for bed each night. The major said part of that was his body healing itself, and that made Harrison feel good.

The day before his second chemotherapy treatment, the UPS truck arrived. Major Bauer signed for the package and the delivery man hauled a big box from the back of the truck. The major set it down in the garage and opened it with a pocketknife. He dug into a bed of foam peanuts and held up a plastic leg.

Harrison's face sagged with disappointment. He knew from the major that the J72 would come later, but he still expected something more fancy-looking than the thing before him.

"It looks like they took it off some crash-test dummy," Harrison said.

"I told you, it's only temporary." The major held it with care, examining it carefully before he waved Harrison up onto the massage table. "Here, let's get this sucker on and see how you do. Trust me, we put a pair of pants on this baby and you're going to feel like a new man."

Coach pulled a tight compression sock over what remained of Harrison's right leg, then carefully fitted the prosthetic leg into place.

"How's it feel?"

"Weird."

"You'll get used to it."

"Should I try to walk?"

Major Bauer chuckled. "With crutches. It'll be a while before you're ready to walk without crutches."

"How long?"

The major shrugged. "A month? And that's way ahead of what most people would be doing. You're strong, though, and you're doing good with the weights."

"Because I have to be ahead if I'm going to be ready for next season, right?" He let his legs dangle together over the edge of the table and they looked good, even the plastic one. The major was right—a pair of pants and he'd be half normal.

"Harrison." The major put a hand on his shoulder. "I love your attitude. It's what's going to make this thing possible. I just don't want you to put too much pressure on yourself."

Harrison felt an alarm go off in his chest. "Why? Is something wrong?"

"Nothing is wrong. We're on track. Trust me, you're as good as it gets. I've been pushing you because I thought you'd need it. Most people do." The major scratched his neck. "But sometimes I'll get a soldier who doesn't need pushing. Some people have an inner drive that doesn't need jet fuel to get going. They're already turbocharged."

Harrison felt proud. "That's me?"

The major nodded. "And that's why I'm telling you that you're doing everything you can. I'm also saying that sometimes it doesn't work."

The words hit Harrison like an uppercut.

"I believe it *will* work, though. I do."

"Then why are you saying this?" Harrison asked. "Is my mom making you?"

The major hesitated. "You mother and I have spoken, and she's got a point. I know we've spent a lot of time together, but she's got a point and I have to admit it."

"What's the point?" Harrison tried to keep the panic out of his voice.

"Just that if you never play football again, it won't matter to us. There are other things you can do—ski, jog, be a lacrosse goalie, like Jeff Keith."

Harrison stared at the plastic leg and probed its metal joint with his fingers. "I don't want to be a goalie. I'm a football player."

"I know, buddy. I know."

Harrison was hoping the major would say more, but that was it.

His second chemo treatment went better than the first. They gave him the right nausea medicine immediately, and even though he didn't feel like eating, he didn't throw up all over the place. He brought his Mac with him this time, and Marty instructed him on how to download a skit from a TV show off the internet called *Little Britain*. In it, two men, dressed up and acting like old ladies, vomited all over themselves and each other. Harrison and Marty watched it over and over, Marty shaking with delight and Harrison laughing until his stomach hurt.

Without warning, Harrison's laughter became gut-wrenching sobs. An unstoppable flow of tears streamed down his face.

Marty leaned toward him, fumbled with his voice machine, and finally jammed it against his neck. *"Harr-i-son . . . what is. Wrong?"*

CHAPTER SEVENTY-ONE

HARRISON CRIED UNTIL THE tears went dry. His stomach muscles clenched and unclenched like a fighter's fists, draining him.

He lay back in the bed.

When Marty's electronic voice asked him again what was wrong, Harrison turned his back to Marty's bed. Marty kept at him, but Harrison said nothing. It was as if every bit of hope had been taken from him.

Finally, he spoke. "Leave me alone, Marty. I'm going to die."

Harrison squeezed his eyes shut tight, pulled a pillow over his head, and didn't move.

He almost thought he would fall asleep when, through the pillow, he heard the clank of Marty's bed-rail dropping down, then the click and sway of an IV on its stand, and the soft squeak of wheels. Marty poked Harrison's spine. Harrison thrashed in his bed, turning and glaring up at Marty.

What he saw surprised him. Marty's forehead was scrunched down over his eyes so that folds of loose skin stacked up in evil, pointed piles. His dark eyes widened so that Harrison could only think of a cartoon alien.

Marty's thin lips twisted into a bully's sneer. He jammed the voice machine into his neck so hard Harrison thought the scar might burst open. *"Get up."*

"What's wrong with you?" Harrison tried to recoil into his sheets.

Marty snatched them from him and yanked them off the bed so that they swirled to the floor. *"I said . . . up."*

"I lost my leg, Marty!"

Marty thrust a crutch at him. *"Here. Use this. Don't you . . . dare . . . lie there. And quit. You."*—Marty gulped—*"Have. Every. Thing. Do you. Hear me? Every. Thing."*

"What do I have?" Harrison felt fresh tears, and he wagged his bandaged stump at the pale ghoul he had thought was his friend. "One leg? Who wants someone with just *one leg*!"

"You. Can speak. You. Can hug . . . your mother. You. Have."—he gulped again—*"A mother."*

Suddenly it was Marty's face that crumbled. *"You. Can quit. You. Can cry. You. Can feel. Sorry for. Yourself. Or you . . . can live."*

Marty turned away and staggered back to his bed. He fell back into his pillows, and his chest rose and fell like the shallow heartbeat of a frightened mouse. Then he closed his eyes and went to sleep. Harrison stared at his friend, replaying the words over and over in his head.

Marty was still sleeping when Harrison's mom came to get him, and the nurse asked them please to let Marty sleep.

On the drive home, Harrison asked his mom why Marty couldn't go home.

She glanced at him and her voice got low. "He's very sick, Harrison."

That was all.

A few days after the second treatment, Harrison balanced himself carefully in the shower, with one hand gripping the handle Coach had installed and shampooing his head almost expertly now with the other. Something didn't feel right, and Harrison looked at his fingers.

What he saw made him shriek.

CHAPTER SEVENTY-TWO

HIS MOM BURST INTO the bathroom. The shape of her figure swayed on the other side of the foggy glass. "What's wrong? Are you all right?"

Harrison held his hand under the spray of water, washing it clean of white suds and a fistful of wet hair. Without answering, he swiped his hand over his head again and came away with another mess of hair.

A groan escaped him. "My hair, Mom. It's my hair."

"All right, honey. We knew this would happen." Her voice was infused with a calm he could tell she didn't feel.

"It is."

"Are you okay?"

"No." He tore at his scalp, pulling clump after clump free until only a few strands came away. He rinsed off the rest of the way. His mom stayed there, handing him a towel over the top of the door when the water stopped.

Harrison balanced on one leg as he wrapped the towel around his waist and pushed open the door. He grabbed his crutch and stepped out of the shower, peering into the foggy mirror.

"Will you wipe it?" Harrison pointed at the mirror.

She hesitated. "Maybe we should cut it?"

"There's still some there, right?"

She nodded.

"I want to see."

"Honey."

"Please. I need to."

She wiped the mirror with another towel.

It was horrible.

"I had a foster sister who did this to a doll once." Harrison ran his hand over the patches of hair. "You're right. We have to cut it."

"Honey, we knew it would happen."

"I was thinking maybe." He braced himself, using the rail next to the toilet so he could sit down and dry off.

"It'll look so much better after we cut it all." His mom dug into the cabinet under the sink and brought out some electric clippers. "Okay?"

He dried off his head and nodded. The clippers tickled his scalp, and the hair he did have fell into his lap. When she'd finished, she helped him up and he looked in the mirror.

"See?" she said.

"Better."

"Why don't you rinse off, then get changed and we'll have dinner. Take your time." His mom disappeared with the clippers in her hand.

Harrison got into the shower and rinsed the cut hair from his chest, shoulders, and back, then returned to the toilet so he could sit down and dry off once more. Using crutches, he returned to his room, fitted on the temporary leg himself, pulled on a sweat suit, and hobbled out to the kitchen table.

He stopped short in his tracks and nearly fell off his crutches.

"Coach, Major, what are you guys doing?"

CHAPTER SEVENTY-THREE

GRINNING UP AT HIM from the table were Coach and Major Bauer, both of them with heads as hairless as bowling balls.

Coach swept his hand over his shiny dome of skin. "You think we were going to let you be the one to get all the attention?"

"At least you two look good," the major said, tugging at his ears. "I look like Dumbo the elephant ready to fly away with these things."

Harrison couldn't keep from laughing. "You guys did that quick."

Jennifer walked in with the clippers in hand. "I hope you don't mind if I keep mine."

"One of us needs to keep their hair," Harrison said. "Otherwise they'll think we all escaped from prison."

"All right," Coach said, "enough talk about hair. Mine's gone and I'm hungry."

As they ate, Harrison had to blink back some tears.

"What's wrong?" his mom asked.

Harrison just shook his head and raised a hand that asked her not to press him. He couldn't help thinking how lucky he was to have people like this sitting around him. He remembered the Constables, their miserable farm, the other woebegone foster kids, and Cyrus, the scrawny, grinning ghoul. His mom reached out and squeezed his hand and he squeezed it right back until he could feel her bones.

He couldn't talk until after the table had been cleaned up and Coach and the major were in the front room. His mom was wiping down the stove.

"If I act funny sometimes," he said, "I think it's because I'm not used to having people around like you and Coach and the major."

She nodded. "Didn't you have friends before you came here?"

"Not like Becky or Jus—"

"What's wrong?" His mom rinsed her cloth in the sink and the bubbles swept across her hands.

"Nothing," Harrison said, even though something was.

CHAPTER SEVENTY-FOUR

THE NEXT DAY, MAJOR Bauer sat with Harrison at the kitchen table, peering down at the eighth-grade history book through a small pair of reading glasses.

"You see? This is one of the things that made Abe Lincoln great." The major pounded his fingertip on the book. "A great man can say he's sorry."

Harrison felt his stomach tighten. He looked at the text and jotted down the answer on the work sheet from school. "Okay, he apologized for slavery in his second inaugural speech. I got it. Next question is—"

The major held up a hand, cutting him off. "Do you realize how important that is? Lincoln made himself one of us. So few great men can bring themselves to apologize—especially in public—but it's why this country will always love him and never forget him. Do you see it?"

Harrison stared at the major, thinking not of Lincoln but of Justin.

"I get it."

"Okay, what's next?"

Harrison finished his work with the major, but when the major got up to make them some lunch, he took out his phone. Under the edge of the table, Harrison sent his friend a text, saying he was sorry and asking him to come visit when he got the chance.

After lunch, he and the major went through a rigorous weight workout before the major had Harrison steady himself on the parallel bars. Harrison stared down at the plastic leg.

"Okay," the major said. "Swing it, on my count. Ready? One and two and three and four . . ."

Harrison tried to keep up.

"Again."

Over and over, he swung the leg, fighting to keep up with the major's cadence.

"Faster, come on. You can do it!" The major's face turned red as he barked two feet from Harrison's face. "Go! One, two, three, four . . ."

Sweat poured down Harrison's face.

"Faster!"

Harrison worked and sweated and never felt good until the final set, a nice, easy warm-down with a much slower rhythm.

"Why the look?" The major wiped sweat from his own neck with a towel.

"It seems like I just can't do this. Not as fast as I'm supposed to."

"Cut it out. You're doing great."

"Now, when it's easy."

"Hey, don't sulk. If I say you're doing great, you better be happy about it. I don't say that all the time, do I?"

"No." Harrison raised his head.

"Then trust me." The major smiled and patted Harrison's shoulder.

The major massaged Harrison's leg and they finished up about an hour before dinnertime.

Harrison showered and put his leg back on along with a fresh sweat suit and some clean sneakers, then waited in his room, reading a book from the Sacketts series. When he heard the doorbell, he sat up straight. He heard Justin's voice and the sound of the major letting him in. There was a soft knock on Harrison's bedroom door.

"Come in." Harrison crossed his good leg over the plastic one at the ankles.

Justin slipped inside and closed the door behind him. He laid his coat on a chair and stood shifting from one foot to the other, looking at the floor.

"It's okay, I don't bite." Harrison pushed himself up even straighter. "Anymore."

Justin smiled at him. "I was just worried, but I get it. I'm sorry about everything."

"I never told you this, but I'm sorry we lost the championship."

"That was so long ago I forgot about it. Who even cares?"

"I know you did, a lot," Harrison said.

"You wanna play something? I heard you got a Mac. I hear there's some pretty cool things on those."

Harrison pointed to a set of controllers on a shelf beneath a flat-screen TV his parents had put in the room. "Forget the Mac. My mom finally broke down and got me an Xbox. I have to read for an hour, then I get to play for an hour. That's how it goes."

"Do I have to read?" Justin wrinkled his face.

Harrison laughed. "Don't worry. I've got two hours saved up. I knew we wouldn't be doing odd jobs or cutting lawns. Yet, anyway. Come on, let's play."

Justin got the controllers, handing one to Harrison before he sat down in the chair next to the bed. They turned on the machine and began a game of Madden. Neither of them was very good, so it was a close game they both enjoyed.

"You got me." Justin put the controller down. "It's good to hang with you."

"You, too."

"Did you really mean that? That stuff about cutting lawns, just not yet?"

Harrison reached down and touched his fake leg; the major called it a prosthesis. "This is just temporary. When the major gets me fitted with the real deal, I'm going to play *football*. So yeah, by the time you start up

in the spring, lawns will be a piece of cake."

Justin blinked at him. "Football? You mean, Madden?"

"No, football." Harrison stared at him, annoyed by Justin's doubtful tone and struggling to stay calm.

"You can do that?" Justin's question was filled with awe instead of doubt, and that made Harrison feel better.

"With the J72 I can." Harrison went on to explain how he'd been measured and fitted for the metal leg and even punched up an image of it on his Mac.

"Cool." Justin took the laptop and angled it to see better. "It's like *The Terminator.* From the movie. Have you seen it?"

"Sure. I guess." Harrison didn't know how he felt about being compared to a robot.

"Anyway, they say you can play? Will you be back to normal?"

Harrison took the laptop back and stared at the J72. "I guess. I don't really know. The major says he thinks I can play. He didn't say how well, but if you can play, you can play, right?"

Justin hesitated. "I really don't know. Hey, that *Transformers* movie is still playing, but I heard it's gonna close this weekend. You wanna go tomorrow after I finish hanging Mrs. Peabody's Christmas lights?"

"A movie?"

"At the mall. I can meet you there. It'll be fun. Oh, I

mean, can you move around and stuff like that?"

"Of course I can." Harrison grabbed his crutches and hobbled to his feet. "Look. I can go anywhere I want."

He swung his legs around the small room.

"Hey, that's great. Let's do it. There's a show at seven. I'll meet you there. Want to?"

"Sure. I'll get dropped off after dinner."

Justin slapped him a high five. "Awesome. Well, I gotta go. I've got to get those lights started at Mrs. Peabody's before dinner. It's a two-day job. I'll see you tomorrow at the mall."

Harrison followed him on crutches to the door and said good-bye. He watched Justin trip and catch himself on the sidewalk, jealous of the way he could. Before Justin was out of sight, Coach pulled into the driveway. Harrison waved and waited because he wanted to ask about the movie, and even though he couldn't think of a reason why not, he had no idea if his parents would let him.

CHAPTER SEVENTY-FIVE

HARRISON SAT AT THE dinner table looking from one parent to another as they argued about the movies. Coach told him he could go and Harrison had already texted Justin about it. Then his mom got home for dinner and threw a fit.

"He's just not ready." She said the words for what must have been the twentieth time.

"He says he is," Coach said.

"He's thirteen."

"I say." Coach stuck a thumb to his chest.

"You're crazy."

Coach motioned at Major Bauer. "The major says it's—"

"Oh, no." The major held up both hands and his fork clattered to the plate. "I'm out of this. I see both sides."

"Both *sides*?" Coach looked at the major in disbelief. "You, of all people. All you ever talk about is 'normalizing.' What's more normal than a kid going to the movies with his buddy at the mall? Come on, both of you."

"Let's let Harrison get a little stronger and a little more acclimated before we throw him out into the world. I *care* about him is all." His mom pressed her lips tight.

"And I don't?" Coach glared at her.

"Stop it!" Harrison startled even himself. The table went silent and the three adults looked at him with surprise. "Mom, I'm going. I need to. Please."

His mom looked like some invisible giant was pressing down on her shoulders. She stared at him for a long minute before she spoke in a whisper. "Okay, Harrison. You go."

She went back to eating, but did so without talking the rest of the meal. Harrison knew she was mad at Coach and not him. When his mom finished eating, she got up from the table without speaking and disappeared upstairs. Coach, the major, and Harrison all followed the sound of her footsteps above with their eyes. When she jogged back down the stairs, Harrison could see she was carrying a box.

She handed the box to Harrison. "If you're going to go, at least you can use this. It came to my office today, so the timing is perfect."

Harrison stared down at the box. He could see from

the shipping label—even though it had already been opened—that it was something newly ordered that had come in the mail.

"What is it?" Harrison asked.

"Go ahead, you'll see. Open it."

CHAPTER SEVENTY-SIX

HARRISON REACHED INTO THE box and felt something silky soft. He wrinkled his brow and pulled it out. At first he could only think of an animal fur, like Lump used to bring home from his trap lines. He held it up, pinched between his first finger and thumb.

"What is it?" he asked, even as he realized.

"A wig." His mother's face was eager with hope. "It's real hair. The best. You like it?"

"I don't know."

"You can go places and no one will even know. With your crutches and your prosthesis, you'll look completely normal. Try it on. Go ahead, Harrison."

Harrison studied Coach and the major. Their faces gave nothing away.

"Yes," Coach said.

"Sure," said the major.

Harrison hobbled to the bathroom with the wig clutched against his crutch handle. When he got there, he took a deep breath before switching on the light. He didn't like looking at himself and lately he had avoided mirrors. His bald head and the dark circles under his eyes made him look more like a zombie than himself. When he did hit the switch, he wasn't disappointed. He looked as horrible as he expected. Maybe worse.

His mom appeared in the mirror behind him. "Here, let me help."

Harrison let her take the wig from his hand and place it on his head. He didn't think it could get worse, but it did. The wig sat at a strange angle, looking much more like a fur hat than a head of hair. Harrison groaned.

"Here, let me straighten it. There. That's it. You look good."

Harrison had to admit, it was better when it sat straight, but there was something still not right about it. It was unnatural. He still couldn't stand the sight of himself, and he hadn't really thought about the consequences of going out looking the way he looked until he saw it for real. He was about to tell his mom that when she put her hands on his shoulders and spoke to him in a low voice.

"You and your father are right," she said. "There's no reason you shouldn't go out. I'm sorry, Harrison. I'm trying to teach you not to care what stupid people think or say. The only people who matter are the kind ones, and anyone with an ounce of kindness isn't going to say one bad thing. I was being foolish, and I think a little selfish."

"Why selfish?" Harrison asked.

She found his eyes in the mirror. "It's easier for me to keep you here to myself, all tucked away and safe, but that's not helping you."

"I was just beginning to think that you were right." Harrison patted the wig.

"Because of how you look? You look fantastic. Completely normal. No one will notice a thing."

Harrison appreciated his mom's attempt at kindness, but as he stared at himself in the mirror, he realized that most likely her words were a long way from the truth.

CHAPTER SEVENTY-SEVEN

HARRISON SPENT MOST OF the next day hoping Justin would cancel.

At two-thirty, though, he got a text that Justin was on his way to Mrs. Peabody's and couldn't wait to meet him at the movies. Harrison spent over an hour in the bathroom, fussing with his wig and tugging on the pant leg of his sweat suit to make it look normal draped over the plastic leg. Finally, his mom called him to dinner. They were having a quick meal of spaghetti and meatballs before Coach would drive him to the mall.

After dinner, his mom pointed to his shirt. "You might want to change, don't you think?"

Harrison looked down at the flecks of red sauce spattered across his white T-shirt and felt his face go warm.

He hurried to his room and tugged a black T-shirt over his head, then hobbled out to the kitchen.

"How do I look?"

"Great," his mom said. "Here, take a jacket."

"Super," said the major.

Coach said, "I'll bring the truck up closer to the garage."

They bounced through town and out to the mall. As Coach pulled to a stop, he scratched behind his ear, the way he did in the locker room before a football game.

"You okay?" Harrison asked.

"I'm fine. You?"

Harrison reached up to touch his wig. "I guess."

"You don't have to do this, you know."

Harrison lifted the wig and rubbed his bare scalp. "I was thinking maybe I'll keep my hair like this, even when I'm not sick. I bet my helmet will fit better."

"Your helmet would fit better." Coach nodded. "That's a good point. Here, let me give you some money."

"I've got enough for the movie," Harrison said, replacing the wig. He still had the money he made from those weeks of helping Justin.

"Well, have a bucket of popcorn on me. It's for you and Justin, too. And buy a couple of those ridiculous extra-large sodas, on me."

Harrison accepted the twenty-dollar bill. "I'll bring you change."

Coach waved his hand and scratched hard behind his ear.

Harrison gripped his crutches and slipped down out of the pickup truck. He hobbled toward the entrance without looking back. He was afraid if he did, he wouldn't go in. He never heard the truck pull away.

CHAPTER SEVENTY-EIGHT

AT THE MALL ENTRANCE, a little girl with a braid in her long red-orange hair held the door for him and smiled up without any front teeth. A boy who looked like her older brother just stared. Harrison thanked the little girl, but before the door closed, he heard the two children giggling.

Harrison winced but kept going. He felt certain his ears looked like two steamed lobster claws and he couldn't help himself from glancing back to see half the people he passed stopping to stare, some of them even pointing. The click of the crutches gave him some comfort because he imagined the major counting out the reps of some drill and the trip to the escalators became a workout rather than a quest for the movie theaters upstairs.

When he reached the top of the escalator, the second floor was empty. He hobbled over to the ticket booth built into the wall and ordered a ticket for *Transformers*. A lone girl in black pants and a vest over her white shirt sat on a stool behind the popcorn counter reading a paperback book. She looked up and blinked at Harrison, studying his hair before blushing and looking back down. He kept going, thinking he could get Justin to buy the popcorn and drinks when he arrived. The ticket taker swung open the big door leading to all the theaters. Harrison hurried through, thanking him, and making fast for the lighted *Transformers* sign hanging from the ceiling.

As he struggled with the door, Harrison heard voices behind him. He let the door go and turned, angry at the thought that Justin might have invited someone without asking him. He patted the wig on his head, but as the two figures got closer, he realized neither one of them was Justin.

Smiling, they came to a stop right in front of him.

Harrison felt his stomach flip, then flop, and he was certain that he was about to throw up.

CHAPTER SEVENTY-NINE

ADAM VARNETT'S SMILE COULD only be outdone by Leo Howard's. Each of them took a turn glancing over his shoulder to make sure no one else was in the hallway, and each of their grins only widened.

"Hey," Leo said. "It's Harry Johnson. The cripple. The Crip."

Varnett laughed. "The Crip. I love that."

"Crip, what's that you got on your head?" Leo reached out and snatched the wig off, twirling it in the air like a mini-pizza.

"Give me that." Harrison tried to snatch it back. He leaned forward, but Leo took a drop step.

"Oops." Varnett swept his leg right under Harrison's left crutch.

Harrison felt the crutch go. He grasped for the handle of the theater door, missed, and crashed to the floor. The two boys burst into an uproar of laughter and backed away, bouncing on their toes.

"The Crip goes down for the count." Leo held the wig up and dropped it to the floor.

"*Down* for the count." Varnett smacked Leo a high five.

The two boys jostled each other halfway down the hall, howling with laughter before hushing each other and disappearing into a horror flick.

Harrison fought back tears. He crawled to his wig and slapped it onto his head before retrieving his crutches and struggling to his feet. He noticed then that his plastic foot stuck out to the side. That's when the door at the end of the hall swung open again. Justin appeared and approached him with hesitation.

"Dude, are you okay?" Justin stared down at the sideways foot.

"I'm fine." Harrison nodded at his mechanical leg. "Can you just twist that thing back for me?"

"Twist it?" Justin glanced at the crooked foot. "Are you shaking?"

"I fell. These crutches. Just twist it back."

Justin hesitated, then crouched down and jerked the foot back into place so that it matched his real foot, facing forward.

"You said seven." Harrison tried not to sound mad, but it didn't work.

"I had to walk. Mrs. Peabody said she'd give me a ride, but she only took me as far as the corner of Route

12 because she was going to Clayborn to visit her daughter. Sorry, Harrison."

"It's fine." Harrison fussed with his wig. "How stupid does this thing look?"

"It's dark in the movie." Justin swung open the door. "Who cares?"

Harrison started to scold him but held off and hobbled into the dark theater, where the trailers for new movies had already begun. As his eyes adjusted, Harrison saw only about five other people scattered in the ocean of seats.

"Want to sit up front?" Justin asked.

"Sure." Harrison didn't know if Justin was saying that to give his prosthetic leg more room or because he liked the huge screen, but after what had happened, he was just happy to have a friend. They sat and Harrison rested his jacket and the crutches on the seat next to him with his fake leg sticking out in front of them. He adjusted his wig again, then reached into his pocket and gave Justin the twenty from Coach.

"You want some popcorn and super-size sodas? It's on Coach."

"You sure?" Justin took the money.

"Yeah. I'll wait, okay?"

Justin disappeared and Harrison tried to settle his nerves. He stared up at the screen but didn't see or hear anything other than the clip of film that ran on a loop through his head of Varnett and Leo bullying him, and him being totally helpless with his stupid wig. He pulled the wig off and threw it at the screen.

"Hey!" someone behind him shouted. "Knock it off."

Harrison just stared at the furry clump lying on the floor in the blue light of the screen. That's how Justin found him when he returned with the popcorn. Justin set a tub in his lap and handed him a cold, damp drink the size of a coffee can.

"Good, it didn't start." Justin plopped down and stuffed his mouth with popcorn, crunching.

Harrison could feel Justin's eyes on him. "Hey, Harrison? Are you okay? Is that your hair over there?

"Harrison, are you crying?"

CHAPTER EIGHTY

HARRISON SNIFFED AND WIPED his face on a sleeve. "No."

"It's okay." Justin's voice was quiet and kind. "We don't have to watch this. You want to do something else?"

"No. I'm fine."

"Quiet down in front!" The yell sounded like the same person who scolded Harrison for throwing his wig.

"Blow it out your butt!" Justin yelled right back.

"We'll see what the manager says about that." The voice rolled down at them from the rear seats.

They waited, but both of them knew what was coming. The opening scene of the movie—two spaceships plummeting toward Earth in a deadly duel—was disrupted by the wavering beam of a flashlight that ended up in their faces.

Justin held a hand in front of his face. "What's the problem?"

"I'd like you two to come with me, please." The manager wore a red vest and he shined the light down at their feet so they could see his bearded face and enormous barrel chest. He looked like a lumberjack.

"Why? Because of some *butt*head?" Justin's voice was loud enough for everyone to hear as he jabbed his thumb toward the man who had complained.

"Justin, stop." Harrison put a hand on Justin's arm.

"My friend is handicapped." Justin wasn't getting any quieter. "And you're going to harass him?"

"That's got nothing to do with you being a little loudmouth jerk. Now come on, before I call the police." The manager's voice rumbled at them.

Harrison slipped his jacket on and struggled to his feet with the crutches. "Justin, come on."

"Well, we're taking our popcorn. We paid for it." Justin kept his chin up and his voice loud enough to spoil the opening scene for everyone else.

"Take your popcorn, but *leave*."

"Harrison, you want your hair?" Justin asked, scooping up the wig before he took the soda and popcorn from Harrison.

Harrison worked his way up the aisle, crutches clicking. When Justin got even with the man who complained, he made a loud farting noise. Harrison wasn't sure if it was real or just his friend blowing on his bare arm, but either way, Harrison's face felt hot. Harrison didn't want to even look at the manager, even when the man offered him a soft-spoken apology and a pass to come back another time without Justin. He just took the pass and kept going. Justin kept right up with him and didn't stop yapping at the manager until they reached the escalator.

"So much for the movie." Harrison took the wig from Justin and jammed it in his pants pocket as they rode down.

Justin raised the tubs of popcorn in the air. "That was just to get you out of your cave. I heard that one stunk anyway. Did you see how many people were there? The place was empty for a reason."

They reached the first floor in the middle of the food court and Justin set their popcorn down on a tabletop. "Let's eat this stuff, right?"

"Then what? I don't want to call Coach and tell him we got kicked out."

"We can just hang out. Window-shop. I don't know."

Harrison looked around. "I don't want to stay here."

"Oh." Justin glanced at the wig hanging from Harrison's pocket, then his bald head. "I get it. Okay. It's getting cold, but there's some benches outside."

Justin held the heavy glass doors for Harrison. They sat down on a bench beside the entrance.

Justin blew hot air into his hands and said, "Maybe you should put that thing on your head, just to stay warm."

Harrison pulled the wig from his pocket and plopped it on like a hat. “Is it straight?”

“Here.” Justin fixed it and offered Harrison some popcorn.

They hadn’t sat on the benches for more than five minutes before Justin pointed at the door. With a mouthful of popcorn, he said, “Look.”

CHAPTER EIGHTY-ONE

BECKY WAS WITH HER mom and dad and little sister. They were talking and laughing together before they stopped in front of the bench.

"How are you feeling, Harrison?" Doc Smart asked.

Harrison's hand drifted to his wig. "Good. Thanks."

"Were you guys at the movies?" Becky wore jeans and her hair was pulled back into a ponytail. She was as pretty as ever.

"We walked out of *Transformers*," Justin said before Harrison could even think of a response.

"I heard this one wasn't as good as the last. We went to *Space Dogs*, for my little sister. Do you guys need a ride to town?"

Harrison looked at Justin, who shrugged. "Sure."

They got in with Becky's family. Becky climbed

into the back of the Suburban and her little sister sat between Justin and Harrison in the second row. Becky and her family talked about *Space Dogs*. The conversation was normal and natural, and Harrison began to relax.

"Dad," Becky said, "can these guys come over for a little?"

Her dad glanced at her in the rearview mirror. "Sure. It's early."

They pulled into the circular driveway of the enormous house and got out.

"Want to hang in back?" Becky asked.

"Isn't it a little too cold?" her mother asked.

"Look at those stars, Mom," Becky said. "It's not cold."

"Nine o'clock," Doc Smart said, offering his wife a hand up the front porch stairs.

"Thanks, Dad." Becky nodded to Harrison and Justin and they followed her.

Next to the fish pond was a swinging bench. They sat down, Harrison in the middle, and stared at the sky. Becky sighed and put her hand on Harrison's arm.

"If you two want to be alone . . ." Justin said.

"Don't be ridiculous." Becky gave Harrison's arm a squeeze. "Look at that Milky Way."

They sat for a minute, just looking, before something thrashed in the water. Harrison jumped.

"It's just the fish." Becky leaned forward to look.

"What are they doing?" Harrison asked.

"They fight sometimes. Usually it's when we feed them."

"Can we see?" Justin stood up.

"There's a light on that post." Becky pointed to a post near the walkway leading to the pond.

Justin flipped it on and the water came alive with a flurry of orange and white as the fish teemed back and forth in a frenzy. "Oh my God. Are they attacking that white one?"

"They do sometimes." Becky peered into the water.

"Look, Harrison. Look at that big white one." Justin's eyes were wide with excitement. "Awesome."

Harrison studied the big white Koi that Becky had shown him weeks ago. "What's wrong with it? It looks different."

"They eat at his fins," Becky said. "But he's okay. My dad says he'll live."

The big, sleek fish was spotted with gray and thinner than it had been. Instead of the sweeping fins that billowed like silk, jagged stubs stuck out from its sides and back.

The horror of it filled Harrison. "Yeah, I get it."

He leaned hard on his crutches and swung them for all he was worth, clacking down the path and circling the house to the driveway. When he hit the pavement, he really took off, swinging his prosthetic like a wildman, but without any of the quick precision the major demanded.

It wasn't long before he heard their footsteps slapping the pavement behind him.

"Harrison!" Becky shouted. "Don't go!"

He never slowed down and he never looked back.

CHAPTER EIGHTY-TWO

ON CHRISTMAS DAY, THE J72 sat propped against the tree with a big red bow.

"I thought it was kind of twisted." His mom stood with her arms folded across her robe.

"It was my idea," Coach said.

Mrs. Godfrey directed a short nod at her son-in-law. "And I approved."

"It's the best present I ever had." Harrison raised the metal leg and caressed the long, smooth titanium shin and squeezed the rubber foot that looked much like his own.

"Should we open the other presents?" his mom asked. "Or do you want to put it on?"

"If he can, he should." Mrs. Godfrey's eyes reflected the blinking lights on the tree.

"Major?" Harrison peered at the old soldier, who sat on the couch in a sweat suit after having run five miles before the sun even came up.

"'When the will is ready, the feet are light.'" The major hopped up. "Let's get that thing on."

It fit perfectly.

Harrison stood, beaming at the four adults. The major disappeared in the direction of the garage, where his apartment was, and returned quickly. He held out a black cane to Harrison, also with a red bow.

"The only present I ever gave that I hope you won't need." The major smiled and scratched the stubble on the side of his face. "You'll need it at first, though. Ah . . . trust me, will you?"

Harrison did trust him, so he grabbed the cane and took a step.

"See? It's not as easy as it looks, but you'll be okay."

"And I can play football with this?" Harrison asked.

"If you can play, it'll be with that," the major said. "Yes."

Harrison tried to move too fast, staggered, and nearly fell.

"I got you." Coach caught him and they all laughed.

The days went quicker with the J72 because there was so much more for Harrison to learn and to do. The shin was a sleek-looking piston that had some give to it, allowing him to spring slightly when he moved. The joints were solid but streamlined; they moved without a click or a clack and slipped easily back and forth as if they were bathed in oil, even though he could touch them without leaving anything slick on his fingers.

The complexity of the J72 allowed Harrison to move with much more ease, and the focus became more about control than about generating the brute strength needed to swing the leg back and forth. Sometimes he forgot he even had cancer, he got so excited. That was impossible, though, when he had to go into the hospital later the next week for his second-to-last chemotherapy treatment.

He couldn't keep from hanging his head, even when he saw Marty's toothy grin and the bright expression on his pale face as he cranked himself upright in the bed.

"Look at. You." Marty gulped and the machine at his neck hummed. *"The bionic . . . man."*

Marty knew all about the J72 because he and Harrison were friends on Facebook. He tried to return the smile, but it fell flat. "I'm sorry, Marty. I hate this place."

"That's how. You are. Supposed. To feel."

"You're always looking at the bright side." Harrison tossed his bag down on the dresser and sat on the edge of his bed.

"The second. To last. Treatment. Is the . . . hardest. The last. One is . . . easy."

Harrison tilted his head. "Have you had your last?"

Marty nodded and grinned. *"Five. Of them."*

That was enough to make Harrison feel bad for moping, but Marty wasn't finished.

"My first. Last. Was when. I was . . . nine. That. Won't. Happen . . . to you."

"You can't say that." Harrison dropped his voice. "You don't know."

"I . . ." Marty's eyes blazed. *"Know."*

Harrison told Marty more about all the things he was able to do with the J72 and how hard the major was training him. "I'm going to play football again, Marty. They said it's possible."

Marty stared at him and blinked.

"Are you okay?" Harrison asked.

"Will you. Do me. A. Favor?"

"Sure, Marty. What?"

CHAPTER EIGHTY-THREE

MARTY WRIGGLED HIS BODY and straightened up a little more. His face glistened with a thin sheen of sweat. *"When you. Play your. First game. Would you. Write my . . . Name. On your. Shoes?"*

"Your name?"

Marty's big head wagged up and down. *"Sometimes. Players. Write things. On their. Shoes . . . That way. I will. Be. With you."*

"Well, you can come." The possibility excited Harrison. "Why can't you just come to the game?"

Marty raised his arm and the plastic IV tube swung and jostled the bag above his bed so that it glinted with light from the window.

"But they always have an ambulance at the games." Enthusiasm flooded Harrison's voice. "You could ride in back and have everything you need and—"

Marty held up a hand for him to stop, and a strange sound, something like laughter, pitched about in his throat. He shook his head. *"You are. A good. Dreamer. Harri. Son. I like. You . . . And. Maybe. You are. Right. Maybe. I will. Be there. With you.*

"But . . . Will you . . . Promise?"

"To write your name on my shoes? Of course I will."

"And you. Won't. Forget?"

Harrison scowled. "No. Of course I won't."

Marty lay his head back and the bed hummed down. Harrison knew that was Marty's way of saying he needed to rest, so he didn't bother him about it.

The second-to-last treatment was awful. He got sick again. It wasn't as bad as the first time, but Dr. Kirshner shook his head and knit his eyebrows and explained to Harrison and his mom that things like that just happened sometimes and they couldn't explain it. Finally they found a medicine that gave his aching stomach some relief, but not before a fitful night of sweaty tossing and turning.

Just before Harrison left, Marty held out a black Sharpie pen and pressed the voice machine to his neck with the other hand. *"I think. You will. Be. Famous. When you. Play. Football. Again. They will. Ask you. On. TV. About. Your shoes. And I . . . Will be . . . Famous. Too."*

Marty held up a bony fist. Harrison bumped it with

a fist of his own, and the two of them held a smiling gaze between them long enough for Harrison to notice the light reflecting off the glaze over Marty's big brown eyes. Harrison and his mom were in the hallway outside when he heard the voice buzzing from inside the room.

"Good-bye. Harr. Ison. My . . . Friend."

CHAPTER EIGHTY-FOUR

HARRISON ASKED HIS MOM to buy him a new pair of football cleats.

"The season is a long way away, Harrison." His mom folded her arms across her chest. "What are you up to?"

"It's like an inspiration thing. You can use my lawn money. I just need you to buy them, please. White ones. Size 11."

"I thought you're a 10."

"I'll be 11 by next season."

"You will, will you?"

"Yup."

The way his mom sighed didn't allow for any surprise when she brought them home the next day. Harrison unwrapped the cleats, tossing the tissue paper aside and using the Sharpie to write "MARTY" in big, bold letters on the toes of both cleats. He set the cleats on the floor of his closet, facing out, so he'd see them every time he dressed.

The major only waited a few days for him to recover from the chemo before he started working Harrison twice a day again for several hours in the morning and again in the afternoon. With all the therapy, lifting, stretching, and walking, Harrison needed the time between workouts to have lunch and lie down to regain his strength. The major was tough on him. Every time Harrison tried to stop, the major would bark and get several more repetitions—or steps, or whatever he was doing—out of him.

Then one day the major clapped his hands and rubbed them together and flung open the garage door. "Today is the day."

"What day?" Harrison blinked at the sunlight pouring in on him as he tied his sneaker tight.

"The day you start jogging."

Harrison swallowed and looked out at the driveway. It suddenly seemed unending, but he stood and walked carefully toward the major, concentrating on his form and the rhythm of the J72.

"You got to swing it just a little harder, like the drills we do on the parallel bars. It's that same quick rhythm. That's why you've been doing those drills." The major held Harrison's cane and used it to point at the J72.

Harrison nodded.

"You ready?"

"I wasn't even thinking about it, but I guess I'm ready."

"You are."

The major stood beside him and turned, slowly starting down the driveway. "I've found that the best way to do this is just do it. Come on."

Harrison flung the prosthetic leg out in front of him and hopped gingerly with his good leg to catch up to it.

"Good. Again. Don't stop."

He swung and caught up, swung and caught up. He was halfway down the driveway when he began to laugh.

"I'm doing it!"

"You are. Come on."

The major turned up the street. Harrison followed. They got to the stop sign and the major stopped and hugged him tight.

"That's as good as I've ever seen."

"Really?" Harrison's leg ached a bit, but he was flying high. "Can we run back?"

"No, no. We walk back." The major handed him the cane. "This was a great start, but we need to go slow and careful. You have to promise me, Harrison. I'm pushing you like I'd push an Army Green Beret, but you can't push too hard. There are limits and I know what they are. If I say you can jog a block, that's it, you don't jog two. Your leg is still healing, and if you go past the point it can handle, you could do a lot of damage.

"Come on, use the right form. Use the cane, too. Here we go."

They returned to the garage, and the weights and stretching and therapy seemed easy. Harrison was delighted and hungry to get back out and run again.

Within a week, Harrison was jogging around the block with the major, and it felt to him like they were flying, not jogging. It was a freedom he'd never experienced before, even carrying the football on a touchdown run.

"Major?" Harrison asked after a jog one day. "When do we cut?"

The major tilted his head. "Soon. I want this running thing ingrained in your mind and your body, too. Cutting is something entirely different and I don't want you working those muscles until the running is down cold. You're getting close, though. I can tell you that."

"And then I'll be on my way to playing." Harrison could barely catch his breath.

"Yes, you will."

The thrill of it all filled Harrison's mind, day and night, and so when his mother walked into his room after dinner one evening, he looked up from some school math problems completely baffled by the anguish on her face.

Fear raced through his bloodstream and knotted his stomach.

"What's wrong?" he asked.

His mom's colorless face crumpled and she tried to cover it with one hand. "Oh, Harrison. I am so sorry."

Somehow, he knew. He just knew, and tears welled in his eyes before he could even speak.

"Marty?" The word choked him.

His mother clenched her teeth and bobbed her head in angry little nods. Harrison hung his head over the desk. His mom threw her arms around him and held him tight.

His breath left him.

An iron fist squeezed his heart, crushing it so tight that no sound could escape his chest.

CHAPTER EIGHTY-FIVE

A CHILLY WIND HISSED through the pine trees above so that they swayed sadly like funeral mourners God had sent in his place. The sun was nothing but a rumor behind the heavy clouds. Marty's father was much older than Coach and Jennifer and even the major, and with him were two people so ancient Harrison was surprised they could even walk. That was it from Marty's side of things, a dad and two grandparents. There were no other friends or brothers or sisters or aunts, uncles, or cousins, and no mom. This puzzled Harrison because to him, Marty had been so open and friendly that it seemed odd other people hadn't felt the same way as he did and shown up in huge numbers to remember the special person he'd been.

At first, Harrison felt angry that the nurses, doctors,

and therapists who'd spent so much time with Marty weren't there. Then he realized that if they did that, those people would spend more time at funerals than they did at the hospital, trying to help people get well.

A silver-haired minister in a black cloak spoke in a gentle voice strong enough to cut through the wind with authority. After he read from the Bible, he said some prayers that he'd obviously said before, then cleared his throat.

"When we lose a child, our burden is doubled." The minister looked around at each of them with bright blue eyes that glinted behind his wire-framed glasses. "Added to the grief we feel for the loss of a loved one is the extraordinary sense of guilt. We ask, 'Why did God take this child . . . instead of me?' But I tell you truthfully, that is not our burden to bear."

The minister looked at Harrison as if he were speaking to him alone and that he might know the secret part of Harrison that felt lucky it *hadn't* been him. Harrison looked at the ground, sick to his stomach with grief and shame.

"I knew Marty well," the minister said. "I loved him, as you loved him, for the kind, passionate, forgiving soul that he was. And if you think, you'll remember his words—maybe even *hear* his voice—telling you to *live."*

Harrison looked up at those words. The minister cast his eyes upon the adults. His words were slow but powerful. "That's what he wanted, and that's what I ask you to do. If you want to honor Marty, grieve for him, yes, but no guilt. Marty would tell you instead to watch the sun set or the moon rise, eat a peanut butter and jelly sandwich with a cold glass of milk, hug each other, kiss, laugh, cry, run, jump, hold each other's hands. . . . Think of him, be thankful for it all, and *live*."

Silent tears streamed down their faces. Harrison wiped his cheek on the sleeve of his coat but never let go of his mother's hand.

The minister was quiet for a moment before he said a final prayer. Then he knelt down in the yellow grass to slip the shiny urn into its vault. After that, he covered the vault with the metal plate that would mark the place where Marty's ashes rested. Harrison toed the grass away from another metal marker and noticed many others beneath their feet, all of them half-covered by the creeping grass and rusted by wind and rain.

CHAPTER EIGHTY-SIX

MARTY WAS RIGHT. EVEN on the morning of his last chemo, the treatment didn't seem so bad. When Harrison got to the hospital, he insisted on leaving his cane in the car. His mother started to argue but apparently felt sorry for him and let it go. He held his head high as he marched into the usual room.

He looked at the empty bed next to the window, then at his mom.

Neither of them spoke.

Harrison set his things down on the dresser on his side of the room. The nurse came in and asked him in a quiet voice how he was feeling. Harrison said he was fine and sat on the edge of the bed in a fog as thick as soup. The talking around him was reduced to noises heard on a city street—hums, bangs, roars, and the murmur of homeless people squeaking past with their lives loaded up into broken shopping carts.

He felt the needle plunge into his arm, but as he lay back on his bed to receive the chemical cocktail brewed to save his life, he could only think of Marty. And that, surprisingly, didn't make him cry. Instead the grief he felt was still so heavy and overwhelming that it simply weighed him down.

Harrison slept, and when he woke, he took a drink and slept again. The pattern repeated itself so many times that when he finally sat up, his eyes groped eagerly for the sight of Marty in the next bed.

It lay clean, neat, and empty.

"Congratulations, Harrison." His mother smiled down at him. "You're done."

"If it doesn't come back." Harrison wasn't going to let her get away that easy. It seemed to him that the entire world was responsible for Marty, and even his new and beloved mother was part of the world, that hateful place.

His mother fought back. "The doctors say your chances are excellent."

"Better than fifty-fifty, right? Just flip a coin." He savored the startled look in her eyes. "Heads, you live, tails, you die."

"Do you want a drink?"

He wanted to deny her that small comfort, but his throat cried out for the cranberry juice in her hand and he took it and drained it without a word.

"They said when you woke up that we could go."

"Good. I want to go. I never want to see this place again. I *hate* this place."

"These people saved your life, Harrison. Please don't talk like that."

"These people pump drugs into your body and flip a coin. Anyone could do that. Who cares? They cut my leg off. They didn't even tell me—they just did it—and I can still feel my toes. Where's the magic in that? It's black magic! It's witchcraft! They should all burn at the stake!"

His mom glanced at the door. "Please, Harrison. I know you're upset, but please lower your voice."

A nurse appeared. "Is everything all right?"

"We're fine," his mother said before he could speak. "Please, just close the door. We'll be fine."

"We won't be *fine*!" he screamed.

The door closed. His mother sat down beside him and held him tight. He struggled against her, but her arms cinched down on him like pythons. Three months ago, he could have broken free. Now, with his thin blood, wasted muscles, and hairless head, he collapsed in her grip.

The sobs shook every joint in his body and, finally, he cried out loud.

"He's *dead*, Momma! He was my *friend* . . . and he's *dead*!"

CHAPTER EIGHTY-SEVEN

FOR TWO DAYS, HARRISON lay in bed at home, ignoring even the barking, growling major.

On the third day, the major burst through the door not long after the sun came up. He yanked on the cord that opened the curtains. They swished back, sweeping up a flurry of dust to swim in the morning light.

"That's it." The major growled and snorted. "You are not going to lie here feeling sorry for yourself *anymore*."

Harrison rolled over and pulled the covers onto his head.

"Kirk!" His mother's shriek cut through the blankets and Harrison peeked out. "What are you doing?"

"Getting him up." The major yanked the covers off the bed.

Harrison lay in his boxers but pulled a pillow over

his head to shut out the noise.

"Stop it!" his mother shouted.

"No, you stop it!" the major shouted back. "Stop babying him!"

"His friend *died.* Doesn't that mean anything to you?"

"Do you know how many friends I've seen die? This isn't about *dying.* It's about *living.*"

"You are out of line, Kirk Bauer. I want you out of his room. Now!"

Harrison stayed still; the silence seemed to last forever.

"Fine." The major stomped out of the room.

Harrison's mom replaced the covers and kissed the top of his head. She spoke to him softly. "I'll be in the kitchen if you need me, honey."

Harrison lay there, just breathing.

He dozed off until his mom came back in to see how he was doing and tell him she had to go to the office for some meetings and to catch up on some work.

"I'll be home before dinner. Call my cell if you need me. I'm just five minutes away."

Harrison listened to her go. Not two minutes passed before the major knocked softly on his door and came in without asking.

CHAPTER EIGHTY-EIGHT

"HARRISON?"

Harrison stayed still.

"I know you're awake, and I know you're not still sick. The chemo is all out of you. I know it, and you know it, so stop lying there. Come on. Get up. We've got work to do."

Harrison held the pillow tight over his head so that his own words were muffled. "My mom said I can stay here. Why don't you leave me alone?"

"Really? You really want that? After all you've done, you'll just quit now? Throw it all away?"

"Who cares?" Harrison's voice sounded empty, even to himself.

"Okay," the major said, "I'll go, but first I want to say something to you, and I want you to look at me."

"Just say it," Harrison said, "or go."

The pillow disappeared as the major snatched it off Harrison's head and threw it across the room. The major knelt beside the bed so that his face was inches from Harrison's.

"Now you look at me, and you listen, mister." The major put a firm but gentle hand on the side of Harrison's head and his eyes burned with intensity.

Harrison tried to swallow, but his throat was empty and dry.

"If you lie here like this, if you quit now, I'm going to tell you what you'll be . . . for the rest of your life. . . ."

"I don't care what I am," Harrison whispered, and tried not to sound shaken by the major's blazing eyes and the angry black-and-white stubble on his chin.

"You either get up with me and work . . . right now, or you're a quitter, and you know what they call a one-legged man who quits? Do you know?"

Harrison said nothing.

"A cripple. A gimp."

Major Bauer stared.

Harrison closed his eyes to break the spell, and he waited until the major finally stood up.

"A gimp," the major said one more time before he left the room.

When the front door slammed, Harrison spoke aloud, defiantly to himself.

"Good."

CHAPTER EIGHTY-NINE

IT WASN'T GOOD.

Harrison couldn't get the word out of his mind. *Gimp.* It crawled inside his brain and gnawed away like a furious rat. His blood felt hot and his skin tight, but instead of driving him down, it made him mad. He threw the covers off, strapped on the J72, and paced the room using the furniture and walls to steady himself.

"Gimp? *You're* the gimp!" he shouted at the door, then pounded his fist against it so that the bang echoed through the house.

Harrison fumbled with his phone and texted Becky that he needed to see her, right away. At quarter past two, when school got out, she texted him back. She'd be right over.

Harrison went to the garage and threw some weights

around, counting out sets and breathing hard and banging the metal plates against each other as loud and as hard as he could. When Becky appeared through the side door of the garage, Harrison sprang up from the bench press he'd been working on and grabbed his coat off a hook by the kitchen door.

"Thanks for coming." He gave her shoulder a squeeze and pushed past before she could get a single question out. "Come on. I need to get out of here."

"We can go to my house," she said, following him down the driveway.

They walked through town together without speaking, but instead of turning the corner at Main Street to head for the Smarts' big white mansion, Harrison led her across the street.

"Where are we going?"

"The lake." Harrison grunted with effort as he silently counted out the rhythm the major had taught him.

"Can you go that far? I thought last week you said the major told you to keep anything you do under half a mile."

"You think the major keeps it under half a mile?" Harrison straightened his back and swung his J72 like the Terminator himself. Becky said nothing. As they walked, Harrison's stump began to ache. He thought of the way the major would get up every morning before light and run five miles.

Gimp.

He hated the major.

And didn't the major say to him that in order to be ready to play football he was going to have to push himself? He wasn't even running right now; he was walking. Didn't Marty, and the minister, too, say you have to live? Everything told him to push himself and keep going.

The sidewalk soon ended.

"Do you want to talk?" Becky asked. They now trudged along on the shoulder of the road.

"I just need to walk," Harrison said through clenched teeth, keeping his eyes ahead. "Thanks for coming."

It was still before most people's workday ended, so there weren't many cars, but the ones that passed whipped them with grit. By the time they reached the park entrance, the sun had faded from yellow to orange. The ticket booth stood empty and the parking lot stretched out before them like a desert. Harrison started to hobble.

"Can I help?" Becky asked, touching his shoulder. "Let me call someone to pick us up."

He shrugged her off. "I'm fine."

They made it to the boarded-up concession stand. Between there and the shoreline, Harrison dropped down onto a wood bench because his stump had begun to throb. Sweat beaded his forehead and his chest heaved to catch his breath. "Let's just sit."

Becky sat down and covered his hand with hers. They looked out over the water, dark enough now to reflect the hills with their barren trees and the fading blue sky beyond with its puffy clouds.

"It's so peaceful," she said.

"Like we're the only people on earth," he said. The throbbing had died down to a steady discomfort.

A crow laughed at them from some unseen perch.

"I think I need to readjust this." Harrison lifted the J72 up onto the bench and began to roll up the leg of his dark blue sweatpants.

It felt damp for some reason, and that puzzled him. The titanium shin had a pink cast to it, and he wrinkled his forehead. When he got to the protective sock he wore over his stump, Becky gasped.

It was soaked and crimson with blood.

CHAPTER NINETY

BECKY BACKED AWAY FROM him and took out her phone. “No, Harrison. Stop telling me. I don’t care what you say, I’m calling for help.”

He growled at her not to, but part of him didn’t mean it. Part of him was scared.

Still, as she spoke urgently into the phone with his mom, he ignored her and tugged the J72 back on, adjusting it so he could walk. But when he stood to go, it collapsed beneath him and he lay in the yellow grass, staring up at those puffy clouds with the shadows of the bench stretched across his face.

Becky was frantic. She knelt beside him and touched his face. “Oh my God.”

“Relax.” He turned his face away. “I’ll be okay. I’m glad you care.”

“Why do you keep doing this to me?”

"What am *I* doing to you?" Harrison knit his brow.

"You're glad I 'care'? It's like you're trying to make me not like you, Harrison. The things you say and do."

"Why would I not want you to like me?" Harrison growled at her. "That doesn't even make sense."

"*You* don't make sense. Stop being mean. I like you for you, Harrison. I don't care about your leg. What can I do? I like you no matter what. I can't help it." Harrison felt thrilled and embarrassed at the same time. He turned his head to the side.

She leaned over and kissed his cheek. "Do you believe me?"

The dead grass tickled his nose. He began to feel light-headed. "I believe you."

"Good." She sat down in the grass with her back against the bench and put his head in her lap. "Let's just wait."

Even with the darkness closing in, Harrison grew drowsy and felt like he could have stayed there that way forever. The sound of two engines grew in the distance until tires crackled on the pavement and then thudded softly as both his mom's car and Coach's truck hit the grass and just kept coming.

Coach and the major—was it the major, or was he dreaming? Yes, it was the major—loaded him into the backseat of his mom's car. His mom saw the blood and cried out. Amid the flurry of his mom's frantic shrieks, he heard the major trying to assure her that he'd be fine.

"It always looks like more blood than it really is."

Coach sat in the backseat too, holding Harrison's stump up, applying an uncomfortable pressure to stem the flow of blood.

Becky sat in front, even though his mom scowled at her as if she were somehow to blame. They rode in silence to the hospital with the major following close behind in Coach's truck.

Coach and the major carried Harrison into the emergency room and his mom shouted at the nurses to find him a bed. They laid him down and his mom badgered everyone until a doctor came huffing and puffing to examine his stump.

"Okay, we need to get him into surgery." The doctor turned away from Harrison's mom, even as she hurled her questions at him.

They put an IV in Harrison's arm. He was too tired and light-headed to really care. Soon they injected something into the line that made the room spin as they wheeled him down the hall. A doctor with a mask leaned over Harrison's face and asked him how he was doing.

Before Harrison could answer, he felt himself floating away.

CHAPTER NINETY-ONE

HIS MOTHER'S VOICE CUT through the fog.

Harrison kept his eyes shut and listened as he pieced together everything that had happened.

"Kirk, what you've done for him has been so incredible." His mom's voice sounded sad but firm. "But you're not his major and he's not a Green Beret. I can't have this insane training anymore. I can't have you telling him he can play. He *can't* play. You know it. I know it. We all know it. I just won't have it."

"He *can* play." The major spoke with a passion that lifted Harrison's spirits.

"Not like he thinks." His mother's voice brought him back down. "He thinks he can be a running back. He thinks he can get to the NFL. We all know that's impossible, Kirk. Impossible."

"Nothing's impossible." It was Coach talking now. "Is it?"

"Isn't it?" his mom asked. "You tell me, Ron. Can he make those cuts you always talk about with this?"

Harrison heard her lift his J72 and drop it on a table.

"Can he carry two or three players into the end zone? *Can he?* Is that what you're telling me? Because if you are, then I'll stop."

Harrison silently urged Coach or the major to speak up.

Neither said a word.

"That's what I thought." His mother's voice was a whisper. "So we have to stop all this. We have to treat him like any other kid who's a cancer survivor. Isn't that enough to deal with? And any other kid who needs a prosthetic; and we have to stop tricking him just so he'll push himself to get better. He'll get better. He'll push himself anyway, but let's not let him get to the end of all this and realize he pushed himself for a lie."

Harrison opened his eyes and stared at them.

"Oh boy," Coach said.

The major frowned.

"It's fine." His mom put a hand on his forehead. "Are you okay? Did you hear us talking again?"

Harrison nodded.

"You're going to be fine. You're going to be great," she said.

Harrison shook his head.

"Harrison, do you know how many kids go on to play in the NFL?" His mom had tears in her eyes. "It's like winning the lottery. You can't hang all the hopes of your life on winning the lottery."

Harrison opened his mouth, but it was too dry to speak. She let him sip some juice from a straw.

"But I had a ticket." His words were a series of croaks.

"Is your throat sore?" She patted his head. "They had to put a tube down it."

He looked right at her. "'Winners never quit, and quitters never win.' You said that."

She put a hand on his cheek and stroked it as soft as her voice. "I know that. You go back to sleep, darling. Just rest."

He shook his head, but his eyes felt too heavy to keep open. He closed them and slipped off into the darkness.

CHAPTER NINETY-TWO

WHEN HE WOKE, THEY were talking again and stopped at the sight of him.

"What?" Harrison asked. He felt stronger and rested.

His mom smiled, looked away, and sniffed, wiping her face on the sleeve of her shirt. "The major has something to tell you, Harrison."

"Why don't we wait—" Coach began to say before Harrison's mom cut him off with a raised hand and the violent shake of her head.

"Because it's time," she said. "We agreed."

The major cleared his throat and extended a hand. "I'm pushing off, buddy. Your mom's right. You've come a long way. Besides, the Army will be glad when they hear I'm shortening my leave. You're right where you need to be, and I guess they got you plugged up pretty good, so you won't be out of action too long."

Harrison shook his head. "No. You can't."

"Believe it or not, there's some boys in a lot worse shape than you who really need me, buddy." The major stood straight as an arrow. "They're probably gonna get sick of hearing me say your name, because I've gotta say that I haven't had anyone as good as you, and I don't expect I ever will."

"You can't make him go!" Harrison's shout was hoarse and raspy.

His mother walked out of the room.

"Coach?" Harrison pleaded.

Coach and the major hugged and clapped their hands against each other's backs. Then the major gave Harrison a weak smile, and a salute, before he disappeared through the door.

CHAPTER NINETY-THREE

THE THING ABOUT THE major was that he liked to keep those records of his very exact.

Harrison let the dust settle. For two weeks, his mom worked from home while his stump healed again. Thin wisps of hair began to sprout on his head, and he loved the soft feel of it so much that he ditched the wig. His mom helped him with the schoolwork Coach brought home every night but wouldn't allow him to do more than hobble to the bathroom. Becky only came a few times because even though his mom was polite, they both could tell she was still mad. His mom put some of the blame for what she called his "death march" to the lake on Becky. Still, they texted each other all day long, and Harrison thanked God for his Mac and Facebook.

Finally a nurse came to help reattach the J72 and give him some exercises that were so basic and easy that Harrison had to work hard not to laugh at them.

"And you're going to take it easy." His mom handed him the crutches, which he took with a nod. "Crutches for a week or two, *then* the cane for at least a month."

The next day, his mom went back to work, and he went to school with Coach, on his crutches. At his locker, he caught Leo Howard and Adam Varnett pointing at him from across the hall. They leaned close, snickering to each other, and he heard the word *gimp*, just like the major warned him.

He slammed his locker shut and walked away with crutches clicking. He had a plan. Harrison was going to ignore the bullies who sneered at him and instead use their cruelty to fuel his determination to get back out onto the football field.

When he got home from school, he found the major's folder on the shelf in the garage. It was all there, everything Harrison had done, everything he needed to do. He copied down his next week's workout routine on a sheet of paper so if he got caught, it would be in his own handwriting. He stashed the folder away. He looked over his workout for the day, then took two twenty-pound dumbbells off the rack; he lay back on the bench and began to press them.

Somehow he didn't hear his mom come home two hours later. She appeared suddenly in the doorway to the kitchen as he slammed home a stack of weights on the leg curl machine.

"*What* are you doing?" She hurried out into the

middle of the equipment, scowling at him.

"The nurse said I could exercise."

"*Light* exercise. Look at you. You're drenched in sweat."

Harrison tugged at his soaking-wet T-shirt. "Just out of shape, that's all."

"Enough for today. You need to take it easy, Harrison. Do you want to end up back in the hospital?"

"No."

"You must have homework."

"Okay."

The next day, Harrison took a detour on his way home. He used his crutches to cross the parking lot of the shopping center where they got their groceries. Behind the center was a long, empty strip of blacktop where the stores took deliveries and unloaded their Dumpsters of trash. Harrison looked around and set his crutches against the cinder-block wall. He took a few uncertain steps, swinging the J72 and feeling the rhythm return.

"Just like riding a bike," he said aloud.

He picked up speed, took a deep breath, and began a slow, loping jog.

He went to the end of the center and back. The effort left him huffing and sweating, and his stump throbbed. He settled down on the pavement with his back against the building and rolled up his pant leg.

Every ounce of him hoped he wouldn't see blood.

CHAPTER NINETY-FOUR

A SMILE BLOOMED ACROSS Harrison's face.

Besides a little sweat, the sock showed nothing. He reattached the J72 and used his crutches to get home, just in case anyone saw him.

In two weeks, his mom let him use the cane. It was hard for Harrison to hide how well he was doing, but he played along. After a week with the cane, and a lot of begging, she allowed him to show her and Coach how well he could walk without it.

"I guess you're okay," she said, "but nothing more than school and back. You do that for a month and then we'll see where we're at."

By the end of March, Harrison's arms and chest had filled in the muscle they'd lost during chemo. His hair was darker than it had been before, and thick, even though he kept it cut short. And, he was *sprinting,* not jogging, *sprinting* ten lengths of the shopping center every day. He kept at it, running in secret after school before he returned to the garage to continue his other training on all the equipment until dinnertime.

The weather turned warmer and the grass began to grow. Harrison begged for permission to cut lawns with Justin.

"Absolutely not." His mother slapped her napkin down on the table as if he'd asked to drive the car. "That's much too much wear and tear. The nurse said it takes a full year before you can get back to normal activity."

"I'm already normal," Harrison said. "I'm walking all over the place."

"For short periods of time. Cutting lawns? You'd be walking for an hour or two straight. Absolutely not."

Harrison looked to Coach, but he only shrugged.

The next day after school, Harrison asked Becky if she could walk home with him.

"I thought you have to work out and you don't want any distractions." She was pouting a bit because she didn't like the way he'd taken to being alone after school.

"I've got to show you something. It's why I wanted to be alone. I didn't want you to say anything."

"Why would I say anything?" she asked.

"I know you felt bad about what happened. You say

you're okay, but I know when my mom said you should have known better and called someone that you took it pretty bad. Anyway, come on."

He led her to the shopping center and made sure the coast was clear.

"Watch." He crouched into a stance and took off.

"Harrison!"

The wind from his speed drowned out her cry. He turned and came back and stopped in front of her, unable to keep from laughing at the look on her face.

"Are you crazy? How did you do that?"

"It's what I've been doing. I've been doing the major's program. It's like he never left. I've done every workout he planned out. I'm getting ready to play."

Becky walked him home in silence. He could tell she was thinking hard about it all. When they arrived, Harrison sat on his bed, putting his leg up. Becky sat on the edge.

She frowned and finally spoke. "Your mom will never let you."

"That's why I want you to help me."

"How can I help?"

"I don't know, but you're smart. Ha. Get it? Smart, Becky Smart. But I'm serious. Maybe if we showed your dad? I don't think there's anything he wouldn't do for you. He's a doctor, right? So if he saw me and said it was safe, she'd *have* to listen."

Becky shook her head. "No, he wouldn't put himself

between you and your parents, not even if I asked him."

"It's not my parents. It's my parent. I swear, Coach is afraid of her too. I've got to do something. Look, you saw me. There's no reason I can't play."

"Harrison, you can run straight ahead, but can you get into a stance? And what if someone tackles you? Can you move from side to side? You can't, can you?"

He shook his head. "I know, I need the major to show me how to make a cut from side to side. If I can get him to teach me, I could play special teams."

"Special teams? Like, another team?"

Harrison stared at her and saw she was serious. "No, special teams are part of every game, like a kick-off. Every game starts with a kickoff. You've got punt teams and field goal teams—those are all special teams. They're a huge part of every game."

"And you can do those?" she asked.

"If I can get the major to teach me how to cut, I can run down on a kickoff or a punt. All you have to do is run downfield like a crazy man and hit people. I could do that. Sometimes players make it to the NFL just for what they do on special teams. They send guys to the Pro Bowl for that. If I can run fast enough, why can't I do that? I mean, I know it's never been done, but so what? Think of how many things have never been done that people do. It happens all the time."

"I don't know that much about football," she said. "I know about your mother, though."

"I can't just give up."

"No, I know you can't." She turned away and paced back and forth before facing him and tapping the side of her head with a finger.

"I think I might have an idea."

CHAPTER NINETY-FIVE

"THE MAJOR." BECKY NODDED her head to reinforce how right she was. "If he saw what you already can do, he could convince your mom that you're okay *and* teach you to cut. We need to get him back."

"Do you think he'd even come back after the way my mom acted? It's like she blamed him."

"She blamed me, too, and I'm right here." She patted her chest. "Your mother is tough, but she's not mean. When I tell the major I'm not scared, I can't believe he would be."

"The major's not *scared* of anything."

"See? Plus, when he finds out that you've been doing his program. . . ."

"He'll like that, I know." Harrison beamed with pride. "He said I was as good as a Green Beret. And when he sees me run?"

"You look fast."

"I *am* fast."

"When he sees you run, he'll know you're ready to do that cut, or whatever it is you're talking about. He'll *want* to teach you, and your mom will realize it's okay because she'll see how far you've come." Becky's excitement wavered when she looked at him. "So what's wrong?"

Harrison ran his fingers over the metal joint of his knee. "I had a mom, a real mom. I know she loved me, but . . . I don't know, I guess she was sick. She couldn't take care of me. She couldn't even take care of herself. Then I had people take care of me, kind of, but they never loved me."

"Now you have both, right?" Becky said.

"I know, and I feel like an idiot saying this, but it's like she loves me *too* much."

"What do you mean?"

"She's so afraid of me getting hurt that she doesn't want me to be *me*."

"Maybe you could just tell your mom that."

"Maybe I should." Harrison wrinkled his forehead and looked at the clock. "She'll be home pretty soon. Hey, want to see some of my workout routine before she gets here?"

"All of a sudden you're showing me all your secrets?"

Harrison shrugged. "I just figured, after the last time I overdid it, that I didn't want to make you uncomfortable, like you'd feel you should say something to my parents. I had to do this. You get it, right?"

"You know I do."

Harrison led her out to the garage. He found his handwritten notes for the week on a shelf, folded in half, behind some bee spray. "See? Today's a heavy upper body day."

Becky moved around the equipment with him. She tried one of the exercises after he did it, using much less weight.

"You're strong," she said.

"I know." Harrison beamed.

He lay back on the bench press, lifted the bar off the rack, and began pounding out reps with the steel plates clanking against each other like a factory machine. When he finished, he reracked the bar with a crash of metal. The work made him dizzy, and when he stood, he staggered sideways and started to fall.

CHAPTER NINETY-SIX

"ARE YOU OKAY?"

Harrison grabbed hold of a machine to steady himself. He liked the note of worry in Becky's voice. "When you work hard, it makes you a little light-headed. It's supposed to. Here, you can help strap me in. These are my 'every-days.'"

"What's every-days?"

Harrison lay back on the bed-sized bench and put his thighs up against the padded rollers that through a series of chains and gears raised a stack of weights up by his head. "The things I have to do every day, not just every two or three days. This is one of them because it keeps my hips and butt muscles tuned up."

He put the belt around his waist and handed Becky its end. "Pull it tight for me."

She did and he began to crank on the machine, blowing air out of his twisted face to get the final few reps.

"Ahhh!" he shouted, letting the weight stack slam down after the last one.

"Here." Becky handed him a towel. "You're sweating like crazy."

Harrison took it and wiped the sweat away with pride. She stayed with him until he finished, then said she had to get home for dinner.

"Thanks for helping me," he said. "I think it's the best workout I've had since the major left. It helps to have someone watching."

"I'll come anytime. I think you're awesome, Harrison." Her smile warmed him to the core.

He watched her walk down the driveway just as Coach pulled in. Coach got out and said hello to her before heading into the garage.

"You're busy," Coach said, sitting down on the bench of the leg curl machine.

"Dad? Can the major come back and visit?"

"I don't know."

"Will you ask him? What if Mom said it's all right?"

Coach glanced at the door leading to the kitchen. "Did she?"

"I'm going to ask her. Because I'm doing so well. He's gonna be proud of me."

"You sure spend enough time in this garage."

"Just fooling around." Harrison tossed the wet towel

over his shoulder. "Nothing like when the major was here."

Coach looked around at the equipment and nodded. "You look like you're getting your strength back pretty good to me, and I like that sweat. You're working hard, Harrison. You can't fool me."

Harrison blinked. "I'm fine, Dad."

"I think you're more than fine." He stood up. "Don't worry. I'm all for it. You're doing everything you can to build back your strength and I think that's great. As long as you take it easy on your leg, that's all."

Harrison couldn't lie, so he changed the subject. "So, what do you think? If Mom says yes, should you call the major and invite him, or can I do it?"

"Do you want to invite him?"

"I'd love to."

"Good." Coach headed for the door. "*If* she says yes, you can do it. Tell him we had to arm wrestle for it."

"And the winner got to make the call?" Harrison wagged his eyebrows at Coach.

Coach turned and smiled. "You're not there yet."

"Yet." Harrison smiled back and picked up a dumbbell.

The outside door to the garage swung open, and his mom walked in.

"Yet, what?"

CHAPTER NINETY-SEVEN

HARRISON'S MIND SPUN. HE lowered the dumbbell and replaced it without a sound.

"What?" his mom asked.

"I . . . wanted to know if I could invite the major back," he said, "to see how well I'm doing."

His mom tilted her head. She seemed to study the wet towel and the sweat on his brow. "You're doing really well, aren't you?"

"I think so." Harrison ran a hand over his head. The hair was thick and soft.

His mom looked at Coach. "You'll have to ask your father about the major. I know he's very busy."

"But . . . you'd be okay?" Harrison asked, blinking at her.

"Me?" His mother touched the middle of her chest. "Why wouldn't I be?"

Harrison looked at her sideways. "Okay. Thanks."

"Well, I'm going to get dinner ready." His mom gave Coach a sharp glance. "No more lifting. He's done enough for one day."

Coach looked like he wanted to explain that he had nothing to do with Harrison sweating like he was, but he stopped before any words came out and simply nodded his head.

She swung her stare back at Harrison. "The major can come for a visit, but we're taking this rehab *slow*, remember?"

Harrison swallowed. "Yes, I remember."

CHAPTER NINETY-EIGHT

IT WAS THREE WEEKS before the major could get away, but he finally arrived.

The rental car pulled into the driveway with the warm sun glaring off the windshield. Harrison ran his fingers over the J72 and hopped up from his seat by the window. "He's here!"

Coach and his mom came out from the kitchen and went with Harrison to the front porch. When the car door opened, Harrison's heart leaped into his throat.

He walked slowly down the steps and marched proudly toward the major without crutches or a cane. The major wore Army fatigues and a tight olive-green T-shirt that showed off his sculpted chest and arms. He cut a formidable figure, like a superhero from a movie disguised as a normal person. Part of Harrison felt outrageously proud to be just like him, a man with just one leg but stronger and more confident than most who had two.

They hugged each other until his parents arrived for hugs of their own. When the major looked at Harrison's mom, his eyes got glassy.

"You know, I'm sorry," he said. "I love him like you do."

"Yes," his mom said, putting a hand on Harrison's arm and squeezing. "I know you do, Kirk. Sometimes I forget everything's not a battle."

"Well"—the major looked at Harrison—"let's see what you got. Walk to the end of the driveway and back, will you? Let me see some technique."

Harrison looked at his parents. His mom nodded. Harrison took a deep breath and strode down to the end of the driveway.

"Well done," Major Bauer cried out. "You look great."

The praise gave him courage.

"Okay." He glanced back at them all and took a big gulp of air. "Watch this."

CHAPTER NINETY-NINE

HARRISON COUNTED OUT THE rhythm in his mind, just as he'd done a thousand times since he started to use the prosthetic leg. His walk got faster, then he gave a little lurch forward and caught himself. He began to swing the leg for all he was worth. He started to run up the block.

In his excitement, he lost the rhythm.

The misstep let his leg get too far out in front of him. His balance gone, he began to veer off into the street. A car coming the other way blared its horn. He lurched back the other way and tumbled to the pavement.

He heard his mother's scream from the driveway.

Before she even had time to move, Harrison shot up and started into his run immediately. The shock of the car and the fall didn't allow him to think. The rhythm was there, just like riding a bike, just like milking a cow, or just like running, before any of this had ever happened to him.

He kept his eyes straight ahead, not wanting to lose his concentration on where he was going. He picked up speed and glanced back to see the shock on the faces of his parents and the major. Instead of stopping, he kept going. He left them behind, running free on his own.

The rhythm was like a machine now, a pump or an electric motor, running hot and fast and smooth.

His feet carried him without thinking into the heart of town. He ran past Mrs. Peabody's house and saw her planted in a wicker chair on her front porch. He was almost certain as he passed that she recognized him and that her hand covered her mouth to stifle a cry. He ran past Doc Smart's mansion on the hill. Becky and her dad were getting into the Suburban. They stopped when they saw him and shouted his name. The sound of their excitement filled him to the brim.

Harrison kept going, up the slight grade, until the brick of the school came into sight. He went right and ran up the street in front of it, past the towering old windows and the fluttering flag. On the corner, a cluster of boys were up to no good. Harrison recognized Varnett and Howard among them. No one said a word as he flashed by, eyes straight ahead.

CHAPTER ONE HUNDRED

FOUR MONTHS LATER, THE lights shone down, blinding Harrison from the crowded stands. Spectators swarmed the bleachers; among them he spotted his mom sitting next to Becky and her dad. Coach offered a thumbs-up from the sideline. No one expected Harrison to return to his original prowess, but that wasn't what it was about. It was about simply being there, even if it was just to play on special teams, to go out onto the field, run, hit, and hopefully make a tackle that would contribute to a win. With the major's help, he could now move and cut, changing direction so that he was more than just inspirational window-dressing. He was a player.

The night air stroked his cheeks and whistled in his helmet's ear holes. He flexed the titanium pistons and stainless-steel springs and checked the rubber foot in its shoe. The shoe—a football cleat—bore the name MARTY, scrawled in big black capital Sharpie letters across the toe, just like the shoe on his real foot. The name stood out, like black ink spilled on a blank page.

Marty had been right. A boy playing football with a titanium leg was big news. All the local TV stations were at the press conference, an AP wire writer, a freelancer for *Sports Illustrated Kids*, and even a camera crew from ESPN.

Harrison smiled to himself, remembering the reporters' questions about the significance of the name on his shoes. The memory of his friend choked him up, but he swallowed it back and took a deep breath because Marty would have been the first one to tell him that right now he needed to focus.

The kicker set the ball on the tee. The referee's whistle sliced through the noise of the crowd. The kicker raised his hand and, in unison, the kickoff team turned to run.

The wave of bodies caught Harrison in its surge. He ran right along with the rest of them, ready to crash through blockers, leap bodies, and seek out the runner, the prize. The pressure behind his face pushed tears free from his eyes, sorrow mixed with joy and tears of love for the friend he had lost and for those who believed in him. The salty taste filled his mouth. Harrison felt it then, as he ran through the night—he felt it, and he knew it.

He was unstoppable.

A NOTE FROM TIM GREEN

When my wife, Illyssa, was diagnosed with cancer, our whole family's perspective on life was changed. Through it all, I was struck by her toughness and determination to survive. Many people look at sports figures as heroes. Anyone who has seen someone battle cancer knows there is no comparison. Thinking about my next sports novel, I knew I wanted to write about a kid who was a talented athlete, suddenly faced with this struggle. Through Mike and Julia Wamp, friends we'd made among other cancer survivors, I was introduced to Jeffrey Keith, famous for his own survival and devotion to helping others. We talked extensively about his experiences, and he became the model for my main character. As a twelve-year-old boy with great sports talent, Jeffrey lost his leg to cancer, but he went on to play Division 1 lacrosse at Boston College. He later ran from Boston to Los Angeles and founded CT Challenge to raise awareness for survivors. In fact, at his request, I have named the main character Harrison and his best friend Justin after Jeff's two sons.

ABOUT CT CHALLENGE

The CT Challenge is a 501(3)(c) nonprofit organization founded in 2005 and dedicated to helping cancer survivors to live healthier, happier, and longer lives. In 2012, the CT Challenge opened the Center for Survivorship, the first of its kind in the nation, offering programs in exercise, nutrition, and psychosocial support for cancer survivors.

To learn more about the CT Challenge
and the Center for Survivorship, visit www.ctchallenge.org.